KERA FAIRE

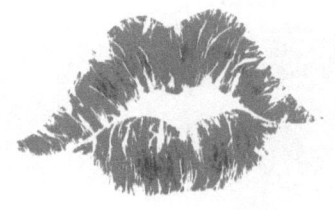

EVERNIGHT PUBLISHING ®

www.evernightpublishing.com

DEATH ISLE: VOLUME TWO

Copyright© 2018

Kera Faire

Editor: JS Cook

Cover Artist: Jay Aheer

ISBN: 978-1-77339-597-5

ALL RIGHTS RESERVED

KERA FAIRE

DEDICATION

To The RavDor chicks. This one is for you all.

KERA FAIRE

THE CARPENTER

Death Isle, 6

Kera Faire

Copyright © 2017

Prologue

Somewhere in Scotland, several years previously

"Department Zee is to all intents and purposes defunct. Over and done with." The tall, dark-haired guy with an untidy plait, piercing grey eyes and an aura of menace about him, stared steadily at Darke. He took a long swig of coffee and watched the other man over the rim of a steaming cup full of aromatic number five roast. "I said and please note, 'to all intents and purposes'. Remember those words."

Darke's nostrils flared as he nodded. "I get it."

"Good." He guessed Darke also got the inference that something was still in operation, even if it wasn't generally acknowledged. "For too long there has been talk. Okay, talk we can take care of. Hard-ish facts, we can't, without a sodding hellish fallout. We do not, I repeat, do not need, want, or even desire that." He sipped his coffee and sighed in pleasure as the caffeine entered his bloodstream, made its merry way around him and woke him up. "Shit, this is good and I need the hit."

"Sweetness and light all the way, then. No

erstwhile reporters dumped in the pigpen you mean?"
Darke snagged his own coffee and inhaled
appreciatively. "No accidental diving fatalities."

"Something like that." The dark-haired man
pushed his plait over his shoulder and inclined his head.
"I must get this cut." He grimaced. "One day. When I'm
given ten minutes to call my own. God knows when that
will be, let alone me." He scowled and laughed
reluctantly. "One day I'll say 'fuck the lot of them' and
retire to somewhere remote I can call my own. Maybe."

"And that's the day I'll become a vicar," Darke
said with a grin. "As in never. So what else?"

"Fuck knows. I bloody don't. However, be aware.
Be very aware. That sodding TV piece was the catalyst
needed, to let it get about that Zee wasn't wanted
anymore. The perfect excuse for both sides. One to
announce of so piously they'd made sure nothing like
that would ever happen again, and the other? What you
know and I know is not for broadcasting. Dark Isle seems
to be the perfect place for what we require." He essayed
a rare smile. One, he noticed, that gave the usually
taciturn man in front of him a moment's disquiet. Good,
it didn't do for operatives to get complacent. "The new
facilities will be able to do everything that Zee did and
more. You will of course head it all." He paused. "And
report to me."

He waited until Darke inclined his head, and then
continued. "I won't interfere. Unless you ask I won't
arrive there. Won't exist. Call it a watching brief if you
like. Without the watching. All I demand, and yeah I
used that word on purpose. It's not a request—it's a
necessity—is that you let me know who is in and who
isn't, keep me up to date with developments—out of the
loop and in the normal way we use. I've plenty of other
stuff to worry about." He didn't elaborate. "I don't want

to have to wonder what you're up to as well."

Orlando Darke pushed himself out of the chair he'd lounged in. In some lights they could have passed for cousins. They were not related except by attitude and intent. An urge to keep their country safe from anyone who thought to harm it—in any way. A burning sense of what was right and wrong, and the skills to see that anyone who disagreed with them was shown the error of their ways. By whatever means necessary. Aboveboard? Doubtful. Admitted to by the government? Never. Did it deter them? Not at all. They were what they were: men and women with integrity. He kept his gaze on Darke and as he had done many times before, wondered what went through the mind of a man such as him.

Probably the same as mine. In, do what's necessary for a successful job, and then get out.

"Yeah, no worries. Mind you, your idea of a watching brief and that of others might not coincide." Darke smiled and showed his white teeth. They reminded his audience of a wolf about to pounce. "Suits me though. I'll make sure you know who the Dispatchers are. Notes to a ghost. No doubt you'll know what else is going on by osmosis."

"No doubt." He permitted himself a brief smile. "That's my job. See all, know all, and be seen or known by none." He uncrossed his legs and gave himself the luxury of stretching. "A shite job, but someone has to do it."

"And where will you be whilst my band of merry men and I torture the pissants and find out how they've betrayed our beloved motherland?" Darke asked sarcastically, without comment on the shite job statement. After all, they both knew it was true. "Sucking up to Whitehall? Lounging on a beach in Barbados, all for the good of the country?"

"Playing tradesman. And watching your backs."

Darke could take that how he wanted.

****

The notes were short and incomprehensible to anyone other than themselves. When you read between the lines of Cousin Jack's very extended gap year you'd be forgiven for thinking he was an out-and-out hippie playboy, with a life of sun, sea, sangria and sex. With an emphasis on the sex.

When you deciphered the code it was oh so different.

Core team set up. Evaluation complete...
All satisfactory...
Eliminated #105P. Strangulation...
Dispatched. # 347x. Pigs—alive...
Disposed. 2213J. Pigs—dead...
Member added. The Furnace Man. Ex Zee.

Intel...

Member added. Mason. Strangulation...
Evaluation of potential Dispatcher. The cleaner.

A+

He couldn't help but send back the pleased...
Continue...
In code of course.
The next email was the most disturbing...
Who is the fish...?
His reply...A cautious one...
A slippery customer...?
Then...
So it seems...
No idea from where...
A message received...From who...? Beware of fish.

Fish... swim silently.
He tapped his nail on the desk, thoughtfully.

Worried. The Fish? Fuck it to hell. His nemesis.

His reply was succinct. *Watch the water.*

Now all he had to do was hunt out the biggest traitor of all. The one who wanted to eliminate them and didn't seem to mind how it occurred.

The one no one could discover anything about. The faceless one. The one who had tried to kill him and not succeeded. He rubbed his side where a thin red scar ran from his hip to his nipple. A close-run thing.

And it was a bitch in cold and damp weather.

Chapter One

Mason's fingers flexed as leather gloves were pulled on and smoothed down, boots zipped and all was checked and made ready.

A ten-minute drive to the bolt hole. Safer than leaving a vehicle elsewhere for goodness knows how long and someone doing the nosy—or good—neighborly bit and setting off alarms about it. As far as the close neighbors knew, Mason had a secret—and it was hinted—married lover in London whenever an absence had to be explained.

Or went to chill out and commune with nature. They probably thought that was a euphemism for hot randy sex as well. Al fresco no doubt. Yeah, Mason wished; that'd be the day.

Mason locked the door and set off. Plenty of time to mentally go over everything once more. It was a hell of a long time since a certain type of talent had been needed and there had been more than a little concern—on Mason's side; no one else seemed in the slightest bit worried—some of the moves might be rusty.

It figured, therefore, that nobody could be happier than Mason that this opportunity had come along. A traitor was a traitor. This one was worse than most. Trafficking and abusing kids—kids from Scotland who should be in school, playing hopscotch or keepie-up with their mates, was to Mason's mind the *worst* of the worst. A betrayal of all Great Britain stood for.

The bastard.

The scumbag deserved to die. If it were up to Mason it would be a long slow lingering death. Where he sweated as the pigs took mouthfuls of him. If it were also up to Mason his cock would be the first thing to be nibbled. What a pity Mason was only a Dispatcher, not judge and jury as Darke had to be.

Halfway along the track, Mason stopped midstride. Could you have degrees of traitorship or whatever you wanted to call it? Surely to betray your country was one of the worst things anyone could do? Along with this fucking child abuse and cruelty to animals. Why did the fucker even have a chance to defend himself? He'd admitted what he'd done, so why not just make the world a better place straight away instead of giving him a chance to plead he was deprived of his mother's milk or something as a kid and deserved to live. And no doubt do it all again. No fucking chance.

That was a reminder. Get the job done. Kill the traitor and let his body be fed to the pigs. Otherwise the pigs would go hungry and who would be guilty of cruelty to animals then?

Mason picked up the leather bag from the ground, untied the boat, climbed in, and flicked the switch of the engine.

This part of the job was always adrenaline-filled. There was nothing worse than getting something wrong.

Not that that was likely to happen. If nothing else, Mason was a perfectionist.

In all things.

One turn of the wheel, and the boat headed out across the loch.

The final part of that night's assignment was about to begin.

Time to rid the country of one evil bastard. Mason whistled softly.

What a bloody great way to live...and let die.

****

Maddock Corrieri. What a sodding annoying name. No one ever spelt it correctly and even that bloody irritating Dori chick who was allegedly his PA had to ask him three times if it was Murdock, Maddox, Mugdock— for fuck's sake, he wasn't named after the local country park—or even Maddie. She was a fruit loop. Dori, not the unknown Maddie.

First a message saying *needed.* Nothing else. Now, before he'd had a chance to do anything about that, this cockup.

Three times damned Dori lost the invoice to send to a customer. He gave up and sent it himself. She blushed, stammered and stuttered around him, until he wondered what it was about him that reduced her to that state. After all, she spoke perfectly normally on the phone and to any visitors that dropped in.

A file on the computer turning up in accounts paid when it hadn't been sent. Then as a result of today's fiasco, he had no bloody idea what the ins and outs of this new job were. He couldn't even remember tendering for it, and he sure as hell hadn't seen the site.

For fuck's sake, he'd remember going to an island in the loch, surely?

Which island and why? I haven't got time for this shite. He'd spent half the night trying to track down an elusive person no one would admit knowing about. One who might, just might, be about to give him more trouble than he deserved. *Hell, it's time I gave this up and concentrated on other things.* He didn't mean getting his cock into one annoying but bloody rousing PA either.

The annoying one had burst into tears when he asked her, quite nicely he thought, with very little obvious anger—except for white knuckles and clenched fists —what he was building, where and who for. She'd looked at him wide-eyed, gulped, and stared warily as if he had two heads. "On that island, a big thingy place that needs sorting and well the bloke sounded angry so I stopped listening."

"What island, Dori?" he asked, semi-patiently.
"What's it called?" He had a 'something is not right
here' itch.

"Er well, one of them." She fiddled with a button
on her blouse, and they both watched, fascinated, as the
cotton holding it in place unraveled and the button spun
in lazy spirals to the floor and rolled into a corner.
Hopefully, if the cleaner had done her job, cobweb and
spider-free.

Maddock got a tantalizing eyeful of black-lace-
covered breast, as Dori bent to pick up the button,
grabbed both sides of her blouse together and looked at
him helplessly.

Without a word, he fumbled in a drawer, found
what he was looking for, and handed her a safely pin.

"Um, thank you." She turned her back on him,
and presumably pinned her blouse over her boobs,
because when she once more faced Maddock not a scrap
of black could be seen. "Ah, you'll know, when you ring.
Won't you?" She stared at him hopefully, like a puppy
wanting praise for not pooping on the floor or something.

*What a bloody stupid analogy. More like a nitwit
actually saying something half-right.*

How he didn't blast her out, he had no idea. Only
the fact that even looking at her curvy figure, and her
free from guile—and the crud women plastered on their
face —features sent his cock from limp to rigid in five
seconds flat, he guessed. But what bloody island? The
loch was full of them. Why was his 'shit is about to hit
the fan' antenna on high alert? There was going to be a
lot of arse kicking soon, he reckoned. Crabtree to be one
of the first.

Bloody Crabtree. Had he ever gotten over
Maddock being his boss? He wondered. He should—

after all the sodding man had suggested him—but now? Now if the reports were true, he'd changed.

Turned? He hoped not, but investigations were needed and no bloody one seemed to be inclined to do them. He'd need to get stuck in himself.

"Madd… er, oh dear." There was a loud crash.

Oh fuck what now?

Luckily it was only a box of paperclips that Dizzy Dori had knocked to the floor.

"Leave them," he said wearily. "I'll do it. What did you want?"

"Um, coffee?"

What he'd give to bend her over a spanking bench and hear her saying 'Yes, Master,' when he told her what he wanted to do. It was unfortunate that it was neither the time nor place for play. Instead he'd counted to ten, accepted the coffee she thrust at him, and smiled—albeit through gritted teeth. As ever, it tasted like coal dust. How could she turn even a pre-packed capsule into such rubbish?

"Thank you." He took a token sip and put the mug down as he noticed she drank all of hers without a second thought. Now it's almost lousing out time so…" He broke off and sighed at her blank look. "Time to finish for the day," he explained. "So how about you go home, eh? I'll ring the guy and find out all the details."

"I er think it's Monday… or was it Tuesday? Oh dear, I'm so bad and you'll sack me and my kitten will have to eat scraps and h…h…help." Her lip trembled. "I will get better, I promise."

She looked so crestfallen, now he felt he was the asshole who had cocked up.

"Seriously, Dori, pe…" Her eyes widened and he bit back the word he was unconsciously about to use. "People will understand, honey, it's okay, easily sorted."

Hell I almost patted her ass, all friendly like. She'd probably sue me for sexual assault or sommat. Thank God I changed pet to people. He'd bet she was one of those who shouted 'abuse' at the top of her voice if anyone ever mentioned anything BDSM.

"What's your favorite color?" he asked her suddenly.

Naturally, the change of subject flustered her. She dropped her jacket, and a lump of what looked like stone fell out of the pocket. As he watched, bemused, she stroked it absently and shoved it into that bloody kitchen sink-sized bag.

"My er what?" She blinked. "Oh ah, um red."

Figures.

"We all have to learn how to do things." *Just you take fucking longer than everyone else and my three year old godson is more au fait with this crap than you are.* "I'll leave a note for you if it's Monday, so you know where I am."

'Ah, are you sure, S... er Maddock?"

S? What the fuck was she going to call me? Sir? Not a cat, or a kitten in hell's chance. Not that he could ask. Lord, she was as skittish as a newborn lamb, and he seemed to spend most of his time apologizing for whatever he had or hadn't done to get her jittery. Another thought struck him. Why did he keep thinking of her in terms of an animal? *Because she could be my pet? Enough already, not gonna happen so suck it up Corrieri.*

Now he just nodded in reply to her question. "Yeah. As long as I've got a name and the phone number, we're sorted."

Dori nodded like an eager puppy on a lead. Or one of those irritating nodding dogs you saw on the back window ledge of old people's cars.

Thank God Buster, his cute as anything boxer puppy, wasn't like that. He was more likely to turn himself inside out and eat the fringe on the new fireside rug. The one Maddock had bought to replace the one Buster had thrown up on so spectacularly it wasn't worth trying to save.

"It's on your desk. I ah, put both his office number and his mobile. And er, thank you, so have a good weekend and..." She stood up and almost hopped from one foot to another. "Well, right I'll er go shall I?"

Hell, does she need to pee? Does she not know we don't have regulated bathroom breaks?

Maddock reined in his temper. After all, it wasn't her fault he either wanted to spank her arse, get out his candles and create pretty patterns on her tits or fuck her senseless. Or, he allowed, all three. She was such a perfect sub, and he'd bet his new flogger she had no bloody idea.

Or that he was the perfect man to show her what she wanted.

If only she wasn't so fucking ditsy. If only he wasn't who he was. If only he didn't have an itch that someone, somewhere, was a fucking meddling, suspicious bastard trying to screw up what Maddock had achieved.

If only he could forget everything and just have a week of no problems. God, he hated the word 'if'. Everything was highly unlikely with Miss 'Ohh um, I have no idea' working for him.

How the hell she ever held down a job *he* had no idea.

How on earth he'd been landed with her he also had no idea. Except Myrtle, his last PA, had left in a romantic haze to go off to Cumbernauld of all places— and he couldn't ever think of that as romantic, though he'd let others beg to differ—with a deadbeat called Billy Chuffin. Who in their right minds held on to a name like Chuffin?

God almighty, what had he done to deserve all this? He paid his taxes, mainly, helped old ladies across the road, well he would if he saw any, and was nice to kids and dogs. Especially dogs.

And serve my country.

Maddock averted his gaze as Dori bent and picked up the suitcase-sized bag she carried around with her, showed lacy stocking tops, and an arse to... *stop that now.* His cock threatened to bust the zip on his jeans as she straightened, and smoothed her skirt over her hips. It took all his resolve not to pat his rapidly beating heart.

Stockings. *God almighty I've gone to heaven, stockings.*

He grit his teeth as Dori flashed him a tentative smile and walked to the door.

"Hey," he called as she put her hand to the wood and began to push. "Have a great weekend. Got anything planned?"

She turned toward him, and once again he was struck by how perfect her body was. Her tits. Oh my, her bloody handful-sized luscious, inviting and off-limits tits stood out, encased in yeah, a red silky top, with just enough cleavage showing to entice but not be over-the-top come hither, even with that sodding safety pin in place. Her waist curved in and her hips flared, to what some might say was too much but to Maddock were perfect. Her proportions to him were everything a Dom could ask for.

Pity this Dom couldn't ask.

He waited impatiently, as Dori bit her lip and let it go with an erotic plop that sent shock waves up and down his body. Hell on wheels, why was that such a turn on? She didn't even seem to realize what she was doing.

Grow up Corrieri. You're thirty-two, not twelve.

"I ah, I'm off to see some friends," she said.

"And, er, you enjoy yourself as well." She disappeared before he got the chance to say anything else, with a clack- clack stumble on her high-heeled boots.

Maddock scowled at the swinging door. There was not much likelihood of that. Blue ball syndrome, as he imagined what he'd like to do with her, was never his favorite pastime.

Ah shit. He might as well sort out this new job. With a sigh that went down to his steel toe-capped boots, Maddock picked up his phone and began to punch in numbers.

Chapter Two

Dori checked her bag, rearranged some underwear and laughed at her romantic inner self. Apart from the fact no one saw her knickers except her—and the cat—these days, why on earth was she taking lacy, flimsy La Perla to an island in the middle of a loch in the depths of a Scottish winter for goodness' sake? Where were the thermals and the long johns?

The kitten, who sat on rigid high alert in the middle of Dori's bed, yowled suspiciously. She knew a trip to the neighbor's was imminent.

Not that Snuggles, the kitten, disliked Mrs. MacLean, anything but. After all, there she got liver and chicken, not tinned food and a balanced diet. It was, Dori had long decided, a cat's way of making you feel terrible and a bad owner. Or was that owned? These days she wasn't sure.

Snuggles pawed one froth of lace with what Dori could only describe as a disdainful paw. "I know, I know," Dori muttered. "It should be the dreaded long johns, thermal vests and a parka or three. Suck it up, buttercup." She'd never owned any, nor was she likely to. As her friend Astrid said, sometimes one needed to suffer for your sex. Sadly, for Dori it was sex as in 'female', not sex as in 'fucking'.

The kitten yawned and curled up on Dori's discarded, Mum-bought-them-and-never-worn, itchy, fleecy PJs.

Dori returned to her packing. She'd have to put something warm in. She had the 'something might come up, so be ready' itch. That could mean outside for hours and a peekaboo nightie wouldn't really hack it. Okay it might be March, but spring never sprang where she lived.

They seemed to go from winter to two days of summer and back to winter again. All in June or July.

Then of course there were the midges. Sodding bloody insects you couldn't see, but by hell they saw you. And homed in to show their displeasure of your presence in their territory. At least she shouldn't suffer those horrible, itchy red blotches in the shape of a map of Australia on her stomach at this time of the year.

Shouldn't. Dori wouldn't bet on it.

Scotland was a beautiful country, she'd agree on that, but hell she hated a lot that happened in it, weather-wise. Why couldn't she be posted to Barbados where she could wear a bikini and a sarong, not thermals and vests? Okay, there were mozzies there, but at least it was hot. And she had repellant. Gallons of it.

With a wry smile at her 'got to have' necessities she surveyed everything she'd unearthed so far. A psychiatrist would have a field day if he saw it. The said La Perla, a see-through, 'fuck me now' nightie, God knows why, her bits were probably tight as a duck's arse from lack of use and a thin strip of leather. Just in case the itch she had translated into action and she wasn't able to use her hands, Dori made sure her gloves and antiseptic were where she wanted them and, with one last glance over the contents, she zipped the bag up, thought of Maddock and how he'd view the kit, and promptly sat down.

God, what was she like? Sometimes she wondered if the silly blonde persona she'd cultivated was more her than she realized. Around Maddock she really was fingers and thumbs. The bloke exuded authority and it reduced her to a twittering, jittery idiot. Why, she had no idea.

Yes I do, don't bloody lie. It was his aura of dominance. All out-and-out dominant male. The sort of bloke you wanted to kneel in front of, call him Sir, and see what happened.

Yeah, that'll be right. Dori thought it was about as likely as Darke would say their job was done and they could all retire and do whatever retirees did. In Darke and his wife Astrid's case, probably make babies. In hers, play with the kitten and knit booties.

Except she'd have to learn to knit first, and Snuggles the kitten was almost a full grown cat. Sod's law as ever.

Dori remembered the way Maddock had looked at her, and shivered. She was there to keep an eye on him, not annoy him and have him give her marching orders, but bloody hell, the dumb blonde act was wearing thin. How on earth could people really be that stupid?

One tiny bit of lace had caught in the end of the zipper on her bag, and Dori untangled it carefully. Who was likely to see her flimsies anyway? Not a soul unless you counted the odd seagull perched on the window ledge. Ah well. She'd better get a move on if she was going to be at the facility on time.

It was a bloody nuisance to have to report to her other boss, do the job, and then ignore him and pretend he was just the husband of her friend and meant nothing other than that. After all, what had she found to make them worried? Bugger all. So why things were going the way they were she had no idea, and didn't like the sensation. Now she was going to have to watch herself all weekend as she and Astrid caught up and Darke did whatever he had to. At least, she assumed that Astrid wasn't expecting her until the following day, and the job didn't take long. By the time she became involved they usually didn't.

Hell, she'd known Astrid for years, ever since they'd played who can spit the furthest at primary school, but not as anything other than a friend. It had been the biggest shock in the world to discover Astrid's 'the flipping wanker I was married to and I'm glad to be rid of him' was Darke. And even more of a shock when they reconciled and Astrid had got in touch with her once more to say she lived in the area and how about they meet up.

Life was full of potholes to fall down.

Dori slipped on her coat, and grabbed her bag and coffee mug before she went through the motions needed to secure the house for her absence. Then it was only a ten-minute drive down the loch side to the camp site, where she had a static caravan purporting to be her holiday home, and she could leave her car without anyone wondering what it was doing there. Even though this was in part a sort of a social visit, she didn't want to share her destination with anyone. That would invite too many questions. Most of which she'd wager would be hard to answer.

Darke thought of everything, even down to the way the curtains and lights in the holiday home and her cottage worked on separate timers, and even the TV warbled away to itself somewhat randomly. A bit like herself. She loved a bit of a warble, even if as her mum had once said, all the females on her mum's side had a voice like a corncrake with a sore throat. Dori sniggered at that thought, wondered what her mum would say about her daughter's dual personality, and leaned out of the car so she could press the button to activate the gate into the site.

She waved to the site warden, nipped into the wee shop to buy bacon, bread and milk and do the, 'I was so determined to get here early I forgot to buy this,' act, and finally after several minutes of inane chatter, reached her caravan. It was just as well she liked bacon, she always had a surfeit. The shop was a bit limited in what she could buy.

Her cream and green static caravan was situated perfectly on the edge of the loch, a little way apart from the other units, due, she was told, to the lie of the land. She couldn't see it herself, but wasn't bothered. That plus a small copse of fir trees helped her to come and go without much interest from anyone else.

Donny McLachlan the warden, was, she was sure, aware of something unusual about her erratic visits, but apart from the odd, 'are you all right lass', when she got back from a job, he said nothing. Did that mean he was another of Darke's employees?

He could well be. Darke had operatives in all walks of life. Some sleepers, some not.

Not for the first time she wondered about who was Darke's boss, or bosses, apart from Crabtree. She knew there had to be some. He muttered about bloody plutocrats and people who thought they knew everything and knew fuck all often enough. Usually just after some almost momentous cock up, by someone who thought to tell them how to do their job. Crabtree he remained ambivalent about. Crabtree's boss, the 'highheidyin' as he put it, the mysterious Carpenter, he had nothing but praise for. "He lets me do my job."

As far as she knew there was only a select band of Dispatchers, each chosen for their ability to kill cleanly, or lingeringly when required. Each with their own special skills, and every last person able to help every other Dispatcher, and in effect blend into the scenery.

She was honored to serve her country in that way, plutocrats be damned.

Dori made a point of banging the caravan door shut, dropped anything she'd brought to make it look as if she was just chilling out for the weekend, and changed her outfit. At this time of day it was impossible to do anything else. She'd dress specifically for the job once she was on the boat.

Within twenty minutes she exited much more quietly than she'd entered and took the well-hidden path to the lochside.

Ten minutes after she'd exited the van she had left the shoreline well behind and steered her circuitous way to the island. Adrenaline had kicked in, in what she guessed was anticipation for the job ahead. Not that she got a thrill out of killing people per se. It was just she'd realized after her first job, the satisfaction of knowing there was one less scumbag on earth was reward enough.

Okay there was always another one to take their place, but traitors and the evil didn't deserve to live.

So here she was, once more dressed appropriately, and on her way to extract a confession in whatever manner was necessary and do her good deed for the day.

It was, as she'd read and heard on numerous occasions, a dirty job, but someone had to do it.

This time, that someone was her.

Chapter Three

"Ah, I wondered if you'd call." The voice ebbed and flowed as the dodgy phone line did its best to make the conversation unintelligible. "It's not that complicated a job for someone with your abilities."

"Abilities?" What was the guy hinting at? Why did he sound familiar? It wasn't a number he knew and it hadn't showed up as a scamming line, but neither was it in his directory. It had been a shit of a day. After Dizzy Dori had gone, a coded message had put him on high alert, and a follow-up to it made him bloody mad. Someone somewhere was trying to drop a person, who, he rather supposed, was an innocent man in the mire and he needed time, more time than he had to sort it.

"Or capabilities," the man said, with a hint of something Maddock couldn't decipher coloring his tone. "Take your pick. Why not come on over tomorrow? The girls will be about and they know what they want more than us mere males. After all, they're the ones who…ah…shall we say, get the effects of the stuff more than we do."

Maddock grunted. This was a bloody bizarre conversation if ever there was one. He'd rung the number ditsy Dori had left for him, and got the local Indian restaurant. Suppressing the urge to order Bombay duck and sag aloo, he'd apologized, put the phone down and tried the other number she'd left him. This time the voice on the other end growled. "This fucking well better not be an asshole trying to sell me a bridge or the bloody bridge will get stuffed up your asshole, *asshole*."

Hold on, now he concentrated he *did* recognize the voice. Darke? Not Dunk or Dank like Dori's scrawl intimated. Darke as in… "Orlando, what's got up your own ass eh?"

The silence would have made a lesser man cringe. With a picture of the saturnine Dom in his mind, Maddock waited patiently, and with no little amusement for the reply.

"Who the fuck is this?" That was what he needed. The clue to show it was serious. Something was up.

"Well you asked me to get in touch," Maddock said, keeping to the script. "It's your friendly neighborhood carpenter. And I might as well say you're fucking lucky I found you. My bloody PA left me the number for The Star of India. I almost forgot you and ordered my tea instead. I rather fancied sag aloo and lamb rogan josh."

Darke laughed then groaned. "Maddock, Mad Dog Corrieri, I wondered if you'd make the connection."

"Yeah well, sadly no," Maddock said dryly, playing along with Darke, now he'd used the beware phrase of Mad Dog. "That numpty left a note, which made it look as if I was to contact someone called Dunk, or Dank. Seriously, she comes under the 'too stupid to live' heading."

The silence this time was enough to send shivers down Maddock's spine.

"I hope you don't mean that literally," Darke said eventually, with enough menace in his voice that Maddock shuddered. "I'd hate to think I had to sort you out, and show you the errors of your thoughts."

"What?" Maddock asked in disbelief. "For fuck's sake, Olly." He used the hated nickname on purpose. "This isn't some sodding made for TV thriller crap. I was speaking figuratively, not fucking literally. " *And watch who you are talking to,* he added under his breath. Why was Darke getting his boxers up the crack of his arse over Maddock's PA?

Did he really hear Darke add 'as well as something else'? What Else could there be? Plus, Darke knew what side his bread was buttered on.

"I don't go around killing innocent eejits even if sometimes I might think they deserve it." Maddock said in a flat do not mess with me tone, and waited for a comeback but there wasn't one. Mindful of Darke's warning, he plowed on. "God knows why the hell the employment agency foisted dippy Dori onto me when my last PA, Myrtle, went AWOL and cleared off to Cumbernauld with some barefoot, banjo-playing hippie called Billy. I swear its karma for something I didn't know that I did wrong in a previous incarnation. No one, but no one deserves someone who thinks a screwdriver is a drink and a plumb line something to hang fruit on." There wasn't a sound. Then Maddock heard a grunt.

"It'll be fucking karma to have your dick up your arse if you call me Olly," Darke growled. "No one, not even my wife does that. Maybe you do deserve that PA after all. Now other sensibilities and, er, employment aside, Mad Dog, are you up for a job?"

How on earth he didn't say 'blow' he had no idea but he and Darke had never felt that way about each other. They'd played together, drunk together but never had sex together, with or without women involved. Not their scene. "Yeah, well, what, where, when and why?" Maddock asked and experienced a tightened, alert sense of that bloody itch at the repeated Mad Duck comment. Something was definitely wrong. "The note and info I got handed as Di... dear Dori went off for the weekend was more than a bit sketchy."

"We've a room that needs kitting out." Darke hesitated and Maddock could imagine the man weighing up his words, sorting out what to imply over and above what it all sounded like. He'd always been one to think before he spoke. Not like Maddock who, until he took his present employment, had opened his mouth and put his feet into it, often with disastrous consequences. A moment with an arsy copper and a motorbike flashed through his mind. The guy was a dick, something that was confirmed when he was dismissed for taking bribes. Even so, telling the bloke that his so-called citation wasn't worth the two pence paper it was written on wasn't one of Maddock's finest moments. Only the fact the copper's radio had squawked had saved him a Glasgow kiss—a head butt.

"What sort of room?" Okay he had a bloody good idea, but for some reason he was determined to have Darke spell it out. Make the conversation more normal? *Define normal? Yeah, maybe not.*

"Tell you what, I'll send the boat for you so you can find out. Come and meet the girls and measure up," Darke said. "The room, not the girls. I've a list of what us males want, but in this case we need our s…ladies' input." He was obviously watching his words, but surely even if it wasn't the 'office' line so to speak, it must be secure?

"The consensus is that it needs to work for all of us, not just some. As we're a right mismatch of bods there's a lot that will or won't work."

"Damn, this line is awful." Maddock sent some scratchy irritating noises down the phone. I'll phone you back." He cut the connection before Darke could say anything else. And made his way next door. To a phone line he was certain was as private as it could be and dialed a different number.

"Secure on here," he said when Darke's tinny voice came down the line. "Why me?"

"That is the million dollar question. Something is fucked up and as you're my boss I want you to tell me what. I think we've been set up. And as a fair few of us now have wives, significant others and kids to think about I need you here to be well, boss, I guess. If someone is after any one of us I want help."

Not what Maddock wanted to hear. "Sh...it... by...?"

"Not sure, to be honest. Someone in pencil pushing land maybe?"

"Crabtree?" Not that Maddock could see it, but who knew what went on in the minds of men who might feel they were passed over and marked as has-beens.

"Not him, but maybe above him and you? Anyway, this was the best I could think of. Seeing as your Mr. Carpenter persona isn't supposed to know about the island. And the room does need sorting."

"Don't you ever play in clubs now?" Darke had been a great teacher when he and Maddock had frequented the same BDSM club in Glasgow.

"Nope. Never. It's here or not at all. None of us want not at all."

"How many of you are there then?" *Why on the island?* And why was he surprised about wanting a playroom? Didn't he have an unfinished room in his own house earmarked for that? If he ever found someone he wanted to share it with. Maddock picked up a can of soda and unsnapped the tab.

Darke ignored his question, as somehow Maddock thought he would. It really was a case of 'well if you want to know, come and find out', and he'd already intimated there were a fair few couples.

"So, will you come and take a look?" Darke, damn him, sounded as if he couldn't give a shit whatever was decided. It was lucky, Maddock thought, that he knew the bloke well enough to accept it was just his way. Reel you in before he decided whether to spit you out.

"We need you. Not just for the room."

Maddock knew how much this conversation had cost Darke. After all, he was one of the few people who knew both sides of Maddock, and was determined never to 'bother the boss'. "Yeah, sure, I've nothing on this weekend." He took a long draught of the fizzy liquid and enjoyed the way the bubbles danced down his dry throat.

Darke laughed. "You better have jeans and a t-shirt at least, please. There's several hormonal women here. They might be our wives and our subs in the main, but as subs, yeah…"

Maddock choked and soda teased his nostrils as he spluttered and coughed at Darke's remark. "Hell, do not say things like that as I'm drinking. I nearly drowned on soda."

"Death by soda. Yeah it has a ring to it. Hmm…on second thoughts add a mask as well."

"A mask?"

"To hide your pretty boy features."

Maddock threw the empty can in the general area of the trash bucket and watched it bounce off the edge and spread a sticky stream of liquid down the sides of the bin and onto the floor.

"Fuck you, Darke." He kicked the can back in the rough direction it came from and swore as even more soda joined the rest. How on earth could so much liquid come from a half-empty container?

"More than likely. Can you be at Balmaha boatyard at eleven?"

Maddock couldn't see any reason to say no. His love life was nonexistent, his Master and dominant life even more so. He could hardly remember the last time he had a willing sub under his thrall. His wax had probably solidified so much it wouldn't melt even if he tried. For a brief moment he wondered what Darke wasn't telling him, but even remotely, the island was under his remit.

"Yeah, no worries, I'll be there."

"Bring your tool belt and your kit box." The line went dead.

So he couldn't argue? Knowing Darke, that was more than likely. As for his kit box? Where the hell was it? Did he mean his work tools, his play tools or both?

He'd guess both.

Maddock picked up his soda can, wiped the floor, and grimaced as he realized the no longer wanted can was a bigger size than usual. No wonder there had been a lot of the contents left when he'd had his fill. What next?

With a sigh that went down to his boots, Maddock locked up the office and took himself to his neighbor's house before he went home. If he had to be at Balmaha boatyard in the morning he'd better make sure his neighbor would dog-sit Buster for however long he'd be away. He might hope to get home to watch the footie, but he wouldn't put a bet on it.

Why oh why was he in such a fucking turmoil? It wasn't just the island and the residents, temporary or otherwise. It was the whole someone trying to fuck him over crap that worried him.

He'd signed up to serve his country and do what was necessary, not have his seniors turn against him and his operatives.

Chapter Four

"This is Mason," Darke said conversationally to the guy who hung naked splayed out and front down over the pig pen, his dick dangling like a morsel to tease the pigs. "Don't mistake her for one of those meek and milk women you hear about. She might look as if butter wouldn't melt in her mouth, but ohh boy." He shook his head. "How wrong could you be? Do you want to know why?"

The guy firmed his lips. Mason brought a riding crop up to strike the bloke across his dangling cock. Hell, men's appendages just looked stupid at times. This was one of those times. Flaccid, and…well, just pathetic.

The guy squealed like a stuck pig as the crop touched him. Quite an apt analogy considering where he was, Mason thought.

"My boss asked you a question. I suggest you answer it."

"Why then?" he asked sullenly. "Because it's built like a stone shit…oh fuck."

Mason rubbed the crop between his legs and pushed upwards. Hard. "Tut-tut. Language and attitude. Say, boss, can't I just get the boiling oil out and drip it slowly over him?"

The guy moaned and thrashed around wildly. "You can't."

"Watch me," Mason advised him. "The pigs would enjoy a little bit of roast prick I'm sure. Or yeah"— Mason paused very dramatically, —"I reckon a brush handle up his arse at the same time. Show him what it's like to be fucked, when you don't want to. How bloody awful it is when you've got a tiny hole and the twattwaddle who's fucking you doesn't use lube. After all he dished it out to those poor kids, why shouldn't he have a taste of his own medicine?"

"I didnae, it wasnae me, it…"

"Bollocks." Darke spoke. Just that one word before he paused and stroked one of the pigs, who grunted loudly. "Your so called partner in crime squealed and told us the lot. Just like these hogs, now I come to think of it. Of course he said it was all you…"

"Nae it wasnae, I never did. It was fucking all him. I never did nothing."

"So that means you did something."

"Eh?" The guy sounded mystified.

"If you didn't do nothing that means you did do something," Mason elaborated. "Double negative. You're a bloody liar. One of those poor wee bairns klyped on you." And to hear the child klype—tell what happened—was enough to make anyone want to kill the fucker.

The guy blanched then retched as Mason brought the crop down over his ass.

"Ah tae fuck that hurts," he moaned. "Gizabreak pal. Fucking agony."

"Good." Mason lowered him until his cock was scant inches from the nearest pig who snuffled the air around it with interest. "Do not lie. I give you fair warning, which is more than you gave those poor kids, the broom stick will hurt a lot more. So, let's start again shall we? Who else was in this with you? I know there was more than two. I need names."

He blinked. "I cannae ahh… no, no more…" He wriggled even more wildly than before. Tiny drops of blood showed in his wrists. As one dropped to the straw covered pen the nearest pig squealed in excitement.

Mason sighed and tickled the pig with her crop. "I haven't done anything yet. But I will do. You see my hands?" The guy looked towards them as she rotated her wrists.

"Yeah, these. I can kill with these in a way so all you feel is a little pain. Or I can put you almost under and let you experience every bite and nip from the hogs, every slit and slash from me, and you'll not be able to scream and let the pain out. Oh, I have ways of making every little thing ten times worse than it really is. It's a hobby if you like. I like to hand out all things imaginable and those you'd never ever dream could happen, to someone who really is a bastard and deserves everything I give him. Up to you."

He moaned and looked toward Darke. Darke stared back impassively. "This is my operative's assignment, not mine."

Mason sighed. "Enough already, I've places to go and people to see. I'll just feed him as he is. Turn the handle for me will you? Put his pathetic prick in line with boss hog's snout."

Darke grinned. "Oh my pleasure. Unless?"

"Unless what?" God, this good guy-bad guy was invigorating. "He's a traitor, why go easy on him?"

Darke gave an over the top sigh. "I bet he was a sap, weren't you?" He addressed the guy, who stared at him bleakly. "I bet someone has a hold on you and this is their way of making you do what they want, eh? Come on, tell us who."

He gave Mason a knowing look as if to say, 'okay, you take over now.' It was oh-so-easy to do. "Tell us why you fucked those kids and passed them on. Tell me bawbag, tell me." Mason ran the crop over the guy's scrotum again and tapped upwards. "You know they call me Mason because I can make you a cement overcoat or a headstone. So make it easy on yourself and spill."

The guy sniffled, pulled on his ropes and swore.

"Ah tae fu…"

Mason took out a knife and cut three strands of rope. Now one of the ties was held together by very little. "The hogs haven't eaten in a week. My boss is about to let some more into this pen. Did you know," Mason went on in a conversational tone, "a hungry herd of pigs can eat a live or dead man in half an hour? Everything but the teeth, and those we have a use for. Do you want to be our next statistic?" The harness lowered a few more inches. One of the pigs, fondly known as Scav, short for scavenger, whuffled as he licked a toe.

The guy squealed and moaned. "Nah, nae more. It were a guy called Teuchter."

"Teuchter? Like not from Glasgow?"

"Aye, thon was right he's nae ain oh us. More a bluidy islander."

Mason considered the options. "And who is he, what's he like?"

The guy shook his head. "Never saw him, just heard the voice the once. Soft and slurry like a Lewis man."

Darke shot Mason a sharp look. "Lewis? Like in the films or in real life?"

"Ah, real life, like when you go there."

"And what did he say?" Mason persisted. "Exact words."

"Fuck the kids to keep them quiet, or it would be my daughter next."

"Bollocks, you don't even have a daughter," Darke said in disgust.

"Ach well, he thought I did and so, and so I did as he asked. He wasnae ain ta tae nae fur 'n ansa." The accent was now so thick as to be almost unintelligible.

"Fucked those kids?"

His expression said it all. Mason wanted to throw

something, strangle the life out of the asshole slowly and lingeringly. But that was too good for him.

Instead, Mason cut the rope. "Ah tae fuck. I'll forgo the pleasure of killing him and let the pigs have their fun."

Judging by the squeals and snorts they were doing just that.

Mason and Darke watched the hogs fight and argue over the body. The shouts and pleas of the guy grew less and less until all they could hear was the chomping of the pigs.

Mason shuddered. "It might be poetic justice, but I wished I could have strangled him."

"Too good for the pisser." Darke indicated the way out of the sty. "Too quick."

"I know." Mason moved to the doorway. "But I'm scared I'll lose my touch. You know, not have the edge."

Darke shook his head in amusement as he took out his phone. "Never. Let me just tell the cleanup squad they can come in and we'll away up to the house. Shower and sav blanc."

"I thought you'd never ask."

They were silent for several yards and then Darke spoke. "Maybe you should ditch the disguise. You know in case Astrid is roaming about and sees you. God knows how we'd explain the biker Dom and leather outfit, let alone the mask, crops and knives."

"You have a point, oh wise one." Mason laughed. "It could be awkward."

"Oh yeah. Let alone how the hell I'm on such terms with you."

"You mean the killing kind?" Mason said with a laugh. "Put that into words of one syllable."

"Impossible," Drake said. "But at least it's not

terms of the fucking kind."

Mason shuddered. "Nope. Not into screwing my mate's hubby."

"Good, so who are you into screwing? Your other boss?" Darke asked in a throwaway tone. "The one who doesn't know who and what you are. I'd love to be a fly on the wall when that comes out."

Dori pulled off her mask and stared at Darke as if he had two heads.

"Say again?"

He smiled. "You heard. What is it with you and Maddock Corrieri?"

Dori sighed, very dramatically. "Bugger all."

"That's a pity, I'm damned sure he'd be the Dom for you."

Dori dropped her crop and stared. Darke stared back, as a slow demonic grin covered his face.

"Up to you, pet, up to you."

God, why did he always have to have the last word?

Chapter Five

Maddock made sure he reached the pier in good time. He'd spent half the journey behind a tractor and trailer, in what locals said 'ach it's a bit dreich', or it's only soft rain, and visitors said 'it's foggy, bloody wet, and sodding miserable' weather. Therefore he was glad he'd given himself an extra ten minutes because the last thing he wanted was to appear unpunctual. Okay, it was an occupational hazard in that part of Scotland, especially along single track roads, but it wouldn't set a good impression.

Ever since he'd known him Darke had ants in his pants over punctuality and he doubted he would have changed. Probably got more anal if anything. Even if nobody except Darke knew who he was, no doubt it would come out—and by God he was going to be 'the boss'—it wouldn't matter a spit to Darke. On time or get left would be the order of the day.

That thought made Maddock snigger, and he was still chuckling as a sleek white cruiser came out of the mist like a wraith and drew up as silent as a ghost by the pier.

A tall blond-haired guy looked out of the wheelhouse. "Corrieri?"

Maddock nodded. "Yeah, you?"

The guy smiled sardonically. "Your chauffeur, I suppose. Hop on."

Maddock shrugged. A man of few words it seemed. No 'hi I'm Jimmie or Jeebsy', just 'hop on'. He hopped and had hardly gained his balance before the boat glided away from the shore. Fucker. Who rattled his cage?

"Electric."

Mr. Chauffeur must have noted his surprise, and chose to impart that nugget of information.

"Guessed so." Maddock reckoned he could do laconic as well as the next man.

To his amusement the other guy laughed. "Darke said you'd give as good as you get. I'm Rio. I work for Darke."

Not told you who I am, though. Interesting.

"Yeah? What as?"

Rio looked stymied. "This and that," he said eventually.

"Clear as mud."

"Well, the boss will tell you what you need to know."

"Sheesh, need to know basis." He did his best to sound bored. As if it were of no consequence. Then Maddock decided it was time to up the ante, and stir things around. Any operative should know what to do. "What are you, a spy or sommat?"

Rio shot him a sharp look. One that sent a beware itch down Maddock's spine. Rio was good. Bloody good. But, Maddock reasoned, he himself was better.

"Or sommat."

For the sake of his health, Maddock though it perhaps best not to say any more. Who he was would come out whenever needed. Why Darke had kept someone who worked for him in the dark, only Darke knew. That convoluted thought was enough to make Maddock smile to himself. In the dark, on Dark Island, known as Death Isle, which was a dark enough name by itself, by a dark-haired man called Darke.

Rio altered course and Maddock leaned against the back of a leather-covered seat and glanced around them with interest. He'd lived within twenty or so miles of the loch on and off for most of his life, but somehow rarely been on it. These days he kept away on purpose. He knew how important it was to appear merely a carpenter. "Does need to know cover where I'm being been taken?" he asked in a conversational tone. After all, surely he'd ask that?

"Eh?" Rio lost the enigmatic look and appeared startled. Then he snorted. "So this is a journey into the unknown then?"

"Unknown as to where, not unknown as to why." He watched as an island loomed out of the mist and grew larger. Big 'keep out, government property' signs peppered a barbed wire fence. "Dark Isle? What the fuck. We're going there?" He never said he was much of an actor, but a certain degree of dramatics were needed in their employment.

Rio shot him a suspicious glance and nodded as he angled toward a cove with a lone pine on a high sheer promontory next to it. Maybe he had overdone the surprised expression.

"Yep, home sweet home." Rio slanted another look in Maddock's direction. "You do know why you're here don't you?"

"I do."

"Care to share?" Rio asked curiously. "I've only heard the barest details."

Maddock shrugged again. "Why?"

"Shit man, are we gonna go around like this all day?" Rio steered the boat onto a gravelly beach and leaped out to secure the painter around a tree stump.

"Well you started it." God, how childish did they sound? "Okay, sorry, put it down to Darke-anal-itis."

Rio rocked on his heels as Maddock grabbed his bags and joined him on the shore. "Hey you know about that as well?"

"I've known him for years," Maddock said.

"Even though we've not been in contact for ages. We...er...used to belong to the same club."

"Ah." Rio leaned over the gunwale and hefted a large box out. "God, those girls. You'd think they could go without chocolate and rice crackers for once. But no, it seems like half are pregnant and have cravings, and the rest just gang up on whoever is heading out. Who is on which side just depends. I've told Andie—my lady—that if and when we go for the spare now we've got the heir thing sorted, the only cravings she can have are for me."

"What was the answer to that?" Maddock asked in interest as he followed Rio up a narrow winding track, away from the beach.

Rio smirked. "A vase in my direction. It missed because she wasn't angry enough, and some caustic remark along the lines of I might be a Dom but even Doms can't control pregnancy cravings. So if she got them next time I'd just have to suck it up." He smiled reminiscently. "It was as well we weren't in a scene. She'd be the one sucking... and her arse would have needed a cushion under...ah, I guess you do know what I'm on about."

"Pregnancy cravings?" Maddock said blandly. Rio shot him a suspicious look and he made haste to carry on. "Okay, sorry. Yeah I know about scenes. I've played a little. Been a bit inactive lately. No sub to play with and no one I've found interesting enough to ask." *Except Dizzy Dori, and I'd bet that's definitely a no go. She'd run a country mile If I even as much suggested she bend over the desk for whatever.* The memory of those stockings made his cock stand up and take notice. *Down, boy.*

Rio contemplated Maddock long enough for Maddock to feel antsy. "Good, so you'll be the right bloke to sort the playroom out."

"Hope so. Bloody hellfire." A large stone building appeared in front of them. He'd been so busy dodging tree roots he hadn't seen it earlier, and he'd forgotten how imposing it was. It was years since he'd checked it out and given it the go-ahead. In the days before department Zee had been set up, let alone closed down.

That itch came back again, and he realized Department Zee was the one thing that really niggled at him. Something didn't sit right. He came out of his reverie with a start when he realized Rio was staring at him, obviously waiting for reaction to the building. He'd better give him one then.

"What the fuck?"

"HQ or whatever you want to call it," Rio said, in a 'do not ask more' tone. "No we don't live there; yes we all have separate homes, though, and do not don't ask in what way; they all adjoin it somehow. And yes the playroom is an annex of that."

"What the fuck's going on here then?" Maddock said, as they passed a side track with a gate heavy enough to withstand a battering ram and topped with rows of barbed wire and spikes, which ran from the gate into the woods as far as he could see. The security cameras were there, but only if you knew where to look. Someone was good at their job. Now he wished his remit had been to become more involved with the day-to-day happenings on Dark Isle. It was all too worrying. He hated going into a situation blind. "It looks like a bloody nuclear weapons site or Alcatraz."

"You might have clearance for other places you've worked," Rio said evenly, "but for here it's this side of the wire and don't ask fucking awkward questions. The Official Secrets Act means just that."

Maddock dropped his bags and held his hands in

the air in front of him. "No need to get bolshie. I asked, you told me to mind my own business. No problem there. And FYI, I am cleared. And I've signed that damned Act." Many years working on the nearby base got him to that stage before he ever went into his present line of business. "You can kill people and feed 'em to the fishes if that's what's needed. Not my business." He bit back a grin as he remembered all the stories that circulated about Dark Isle. That it was now Death Isle, that if you went there you'd never be seen again and that naked witches danced around it at midnight. Actually the naked bit was the one thing he thought most locals decided were plausible. The rest would probably seem like the ideas conjured up after one too many magic mushrooms.

Rio snorted. "Only traitors, and to the pigs. You'll be safe."

Chapter Six

"That's okay then. So," Maddock picked up his bags, "show me the way, then we can get it done and I can get into the city. There's an old firm game on I want to avoid so I want to be in and out while the match is on, not before or after. Then I can watch it with a few beers from the safely of my armchair."

"Er, I think Darke might have an idea about that," Rio said. "I got the impression you're here for the weekend. Well, there's a room made up for you and Astrid and Mason were talking about who shouldn't make dinner."

"Shouldn't?"

Rio snorted. "Let's just say the level of cookery skills vary considerably. I guess that's why it's dinner at the big house and Michael is cooking. He's not long been seconded here, but boy can he cook. Took a long while to admit it though. Bastard." Rio whistled through his teeth. "'Hopefully it's spag... oh fuck." His expression was comically dismayed. "Shall I tell him we've got an Italiano here and skip the spag?"

"Oh God, no. As long as I don't have to cook the stuff I love pasta. Just never got the hang of it. I'm a meat and two veg man myself." The minute the words left his mouth, Maddock wished he could call them back. Rio stared at his face, then his crotch, and then back to his face again.

"Hmm, I can see that."

"I guess I asked for that," Maddock said ruefully. "But it's better than saying deep fried pizza."

Rio shuddered theatrically. "True enough."

They reached the imposing front door of what Maddock was sure he'd read—'before'—was an old laird's house, probably built around the end of the eighteenth century. Rio hefted it open and stood back. "Welcome to well, whatever, I guess. Darke said to show you to his office. It's down here."

Maddock followed him along a wide, light corridor. The outside of the building might be old, but the inside wasn't.

Rio tapped on a blank uninformative door to their left and opened it. "Hey boss, here's the carpenter." He stood back to let Maddock enter, and sketched a wave. "I'll drop the bags off, then head to the comms room. That's where I'll be if I'm needed."

Maddock walked slowly into the room, and once the door closed behind Rio, stared at Darke.

"So." He waited, not sure whether to be amused or pissed at all the subterfuge.

"So?" Darke parroted. "So, boss man, what the fuck's going on?"

"I hoped you were going to tell me that." Maddock picked up a hard-backed chair from near the wall, turned it around and sat astride. He crossed his arms on the top of the back and rested his chin on his hands. His thinking pose. "Our remit didn't say anything about visits here to meet up. In fact I distinctly remember telling you I wasn't to be approached unless it was urgent and critical."

Dare shrugged. "Boss man, it's urgent and critical. I need you."

"What?" Maddock rocked in his chair. "That's some admission coming from you. How about specifics?"

"Yeah." Darke ran his hand through his hair. "Something dirty is going down. I got a message saying I was to expect a new parcel. No details of who was bringing it. So I did a bit of digging. Someone is trying to say Department Zee is still ongoing and heads need to roll. Now the Intel said no more, and the message came all official like from someone at...." He hesitated. "You know where." It was strange but not unexpected how neither of them ever mentioned where that top secret place was.

"Yeah, so what was the problem?"

"You weren't copied in, nor was Crabtree. Well, as they're trying to implicate him, I guess that's understandable. But why not you? And when I got Michael, who is a whiz on computers to do a bit of hacking, it came from the personal laptop of one Jackson. Who is dead."

"Fuck." Jackson had been one of the assholes who had not that long ago tried to kidnap Astrid, and Maddock had discounted him…and his electronics. "So it's still 'let's get Crabtree; then?" He knew part of the answer but wondered what information Darke was privy to.

"So it seems, but why? We still have no answer to that. To coin a phrase my wife is keen on, it sucks donkey balls." Darke shook his head in disgust. "Sodding awful expression but boy, it sums up how I feel about the situation."

That it did. "And the package?" Maddock asked. He had a bad, bad feeling about all this.

"I still have no idea how the package is arriving but I've reason to believe it could be Crabtree."

That was the last thing Maddock expected to hear. "What? Crabtree is the parcel? Never." Maddock stood up and began to pace. "Not Crabtree. Why are they trying to discredit him again? I mean anyone with a little gumption wouldn't go for him turning. He's as straight as a telegraph pole. One of the few people I'd say was a loyal citizen to the core. Never a traitor."

"Of course he's not. I bloody hope you'd never think that. He works for you, for Christ's sake." Darke stared at Maddock broodingly. "And he's Astrid's dad."

Maddock nodded. "Yeah I know."

"You know?" Darke's eyes flared in astonishment before he swiftly masked the emotion.

It seemed Darke could still be surprised.

Maddock shrugged nonchalantly. "I know everything. Well," he amended, "almost everything. I was only ever here to keep a distant eye on what's going on, as you know. My remit was an overall watching brief of…well let's just say of a much wider area."

"The info I've had is that somebody or bodies involved in that attempted abduction of Astrid are on the move," Darke said. "After that screw-up, everything went quiet, but now someone is stirring. No names, no info, except it could be tied in with Crabtree. But I ignored that bit because I know the man. Mind you I thought I knew Jackson as well. What a fucking mess."

"Well if it is what next I wonder?"

Darke groaned. "Hell, I—or you—don't tell Astrid, she's antsy enough as it is. For fuck's sake show you're here to sort the playroom and let's dig later. All I will say is why now? Ever since they disbanded Dep—" He shot a quick look at Maddock and rolled his eyes. "Okay, no more but hell, *boss,* you know what I mean."

Sadly he did. "Yup, and so later we'll have a meeting. Anyone else you think needs to be in on it?"

He could see the cogs rolling, as Darke thought fast. "Hmm, well, as it tends to be all or no one, I'd say no one at first. Then, up to you. This is one time I'm glad to hand over responsibility."

Maddock grunted. "Coffee then, before I look at the room. Lucky I really do know what I'm doing eh?"

There was a tap at the door and both men turned

toward it. Rio appeared, "Boss, the bags are in Maddock's room, and Michael says lunch in an hour. And when you have a sec, can you come to the ops room and check out those new lines with me. I'm not happy with them."

Darke inclined his head. "Will do. Can you take Maddock and show him the playroom to be, and I'll catch you up once I've checked on something?"

Rio blinked. "I thought that was the girls' job. The playroom, I mean."

"I thought we might get a head start," Darke said gravely.

Rio grinned. "You're feeling brave," he said. "And I'm not owning up to having any part of it."

"Wuss. Ah…fuck." The phone rang. "Go on, you take Maddock and I'll join you."

Rio glanced at Maddock and winked. "You up for it?"

"Why not? I *can* plead ignorance and mean it." Maddock followed Rio out of the room, and listened, amused, as Darke began to bark questions down the phone. It seemed someone had annoyed him. He'd find out why later.

As they retraced their steps, Rio waved to a door on their left. "That takes you into the annex where the playroom is going to be. Also the guest bedrooms. For those guests that are welcomed. Not a lot to be honest. You're in the room first left. Communal dining room here, which we don't use that often and well, hi, ladies, what you up to?" Two women backed out of the dining room. "Got jankers have we? What have you been doing you shouldn't or is it best I not ask?"

"Bugger all, we just didn't hide fast enough," the first one—clad in dungarees and a shocking pink t-shirt—said humorously as she turned around and looked from Rio to Maddock. "Hi I'm Astrid, Darke's better half. This is the rear view of Mason, my mate." She tugged on a long blonde plait. "Mase, be nice and don't growl at the gentlemen. Not all men are assholes. Just some of them."

With a gentle swirl of a long multicolored ruffled skirt, Mason turned slowly, looked at them both and paled. Her arms were bare, her chest covered in a thin short sleeved sweater and her hands were full of glass casseroles and plates. They wobbled.

Maddock stared. "Fucking hell, Dori?"

Glass and pottery went all over the place.

Chapter Seven

Why wasn't there a great big hole around when you needed one? Dori stared at the guy in front of her and cursed. His expression changed from incredulous, to thunderous, to wary.

"Of all the guys on all the islands in all the world," she paraphrased desperately, and did her best to ignore the glint in his eyes. Retribution was on its way she was sure of it, and she was certain that no one would help her sidestep it. "I have to meet you." She realized what she said, dug her fingers into her wrists, and fought against her natural instinct to bow her head.

Rio fucking laughed, and Dori scowled at him. "Why are you here?" she said to Maddock, not exactly politely. "Er... I mean...."

God, that look. If anything was guaranteed to make her go down on her knees it was. Out-and-out dominant. Bloody hell. Wet knicker alert.

"He is here to plan our playroom." Darke had appeared as silently as he often did. A swift, complicated glance passed between him and Maddock. One she couldn't interpret. "Astrid, you're needed in the office. Rio, the alarm is playing up."

Rio opened his mouth and shut it with a snap. "Yeah, okay." He disappeared with alacrity. Two seconds later he reappeared. "Who pinched the screwdrivers?"

"Eh? Hold on." Darke turned to where Astrid hovered.

"Pet."

She sighed and scowled. "Oh all *right*, but we are not in a scene and I think I need to be here. You know, as an impartial witness."

Darke raised his eyebrow. "Define impartial."

Astrid sniggered. "On her side of course, even it up. Two or is it three against one isn't fair in normal circumstances let alone with faces like thunder. What, *Sir,* is going on?" Her voice rose. "Darke, please."

Darke's grim expression faded as he stroked Astrid's cheek. "It's all right, pet. We just have things to sort out. Mason will be with you before you know it. Go and categorize this week's paperwork for me in the office, please. After all"— a quick, un-Darke like smile flashed across his face— "I best not ask Mason to do it."

"Oh, okay." Astrid rolled her eyes and scowled. "But it still doesn't seem fair."

"Believe me it is." He kissed her with relish and she returned the embrace so fervently, Dori wondered if she was supposed to shut her eyes or give them marks out of ten.

Maddock seemed to have no qualms about interrupting. "Do we go out, knock and cough loudly?"

Rio snorted. "You'd get dizzy if you did that every time they got jiggy."

Darke lifted his head. "Pot and kettle maybe…?" He patted Astrid's bottom. "The office awaits."

"Yeah yeah. Shout if you need me, Mase. I'll come running with my pen held like a spear." She didn't move. "Or I can wait."

Darke shrugged. "No, you cannot. Move. So, Mad Dog? Now?"

Maddock smiled. "I guess it's your call."

Mason wondered what that all meant. Or she would have if there weren't enough on her mind at that moment. She looked toward Darke who cleared his throat as a hint he needed her attention.

"Mason, you need to show our guest to his room and then to the playroom. I'll meet you there later. The plans are on the bench." He paused and did that sodding one raised eyebrow thing that Dori bloody hated.

"Food in two hours. Use the time wisely." Darke grabbed Astrid's arm and dragged her behind him.

"Wha…?" Dori watched in bemusement, as Darke flung Astrid over his shoulder and said something to her no one else could hear. She raised her head and winked at Dori before she mouthed 'good luck'.

Rio let out one sharp bark of laughter and stared from Dori to Maddock. "I'm not even going to ask." He sketched a sarcastic bow. "I'd say enjoy yourselves but yeah well. Remember the playroom. I'm off to hunt screwdrivers and sort wires. Make sure you don't get yours crossed." He turned on his heel.

The silence in the corridor was deafening. Eventually, Dori lifted her gaze. And wished she hadn't. Maddock was looking at her in such a way she knew, just knew, he wished he had a flogger and the permission to use it.

"Clear as muck," he said sardonically. "Why does everyone talk in bloody riddles here?"

Dori shrugged. No answer sprang to mind. None that made sense or didn't compromise who and what she was, anyway.

"So, do I call you Mason or Dori?" Maddock said, just as she was ready to scream 'say something, say anything' at him. "Because I'm sure you will appreciate I like to know who I'm…" He stared at her so long she did that stupid leg hopping crap she had done in the office. What was it with Maddock that turned her into a klutz? Seriously, it was bad enough having every aroused nerve screaming touch me, play with me, without looking like a right galoot.

"Talking to," he finished finally. "And whatever else transpires."

"Er well, up to you. I'm er, well..." *Shut up Dori. Just shut up.* She bent down and picked up the nearest large bits of shattered glass and pottery. The rest she'd need to take a broom to.

"Tell me." His words were staccato and peremptory. It was enough to send her angry levels off the range.

Dori stopped mid-bend and promptly dropped the shards again. At this rate she'd be sweeping up splinters for a week. Instead of increasing her klutz ratio, it made her even more mad. How dare he come over to the island upset her 'cool and calm after the job has been successfully done' mood and act like her Sir. Fuck that. That she was behaving totally irrationally and over the top in response to his actions she didn't even consider. It was about time she had a good mad.

"Stop bloody barking orders at me," she said angrily. "I'm not your sodding sub, and don't you forget it."

"No?" Maddock said in that knicker dampening tone he did so well. "Then what are you sweetness, eh? Because you're sure as hell not a PA. One of the weirdoes that live here?"

What? How dare he call her friends and colleagues weirdoes? She threw what pottery she still held in his direction, took one look at his thunderous face and legged it.

Where to go? Dori had no idea and turned through the first open doorway she came to. Panting, she slammed it shut and did her best to lean on it and keep him out.

Of course she failed.

Maddock pushed the wood, moved her to one side as if she were a feather and stalked into the room.

To her annoyance, the bugger laughed. "Well,

well, what's this, sweetness? A Freudian slip? Because if my eyes don't deceive me that's a spanking bench over there, and ohh my, some nice new handcuffs next to it."

Hell on wheels. Dori closed her eyes. What imp of mischief decreed it was the playroom she rushed into? She moved away from him carefully—or so she thought—tripped over nothing and her footwear flew off. Why had she put on flip flops when she and Astrid had chatted earlier? They usually went barefoot, but David, one of the Dispatchers was also a heating engineer, was doing an overhaul. As neither she nor Astrid had slippers she'd borrowed a pair of Astrid's flip flops, which were two sizes too big.

Maddock shackled one of her wrists in his hand and dragged her—literally dragged her, with her toes rubbing the floor—across the room. "Ah yes, I'd forgotten Darke knows my preferences. There's some nice new wax here. Does he think we're ready to play?"

"What? No," she said desperately. Oh she wanted do, but not now, not until she had rid herself of the memories of her last job. Got the horrible taste of work out of her mouth and regained her inner balance. "Why on earth would he?" Darke knew it took her several days to snap out of the brutality of their jobs. Everyone reacted differently. She was sure some of the other Dispatchers went home and fucked their partners like rabbits to celebrate their life. Whether or not to create new lives was a moot point, even though there had been a lot of jokes about how the island should be renamed Fertility Isle due to the number of babies and pregnancies amongst the Dispatchers' families.

Rio, to the amusement of the others, had learned to crochet and Michael had decided to learn to play the cello. Dori went for a hot scented bath and then played with her chisels and stone. Many an ornamental gargoyle has been created in the aftermath of an execution.

"I don't know," Maddock said softly, but in a voice tinged with steel that dragged her thoughts back to him. "Why would he think we'd be the perfect pair? You tell me."

Dori listened to her heart thudding. She was dropped well into it now. No doubt Darke has some reasoning behind his actions, but oh boy, why hadn't he let her in on the secret?

"Waiting, pet. And do not dare to insult my intelligence and say you're not a sub."

"I wouldn't dream of it," she said indignantly, "But I'm not *your* sub."

"Ah, but you'd like to be." It wasn't a question.

"I don't know," Dori said eventually. "How could I?"

Maddock raised one eyebrow. *Damn him that does get my inner sub channeling like crazy, and I bet he knows it.*

"Hmm. Now everything falls into place, I could say how couldn't you?" he paused. "Pet."

He had a point. However, it wasn't in her nature to give in easily. "Because I'm not?" She'd hadn't meant it to sound like a question, or to speak in such a breathy, submissive voice, but it seemed her inner sub wasn't going to let her get away that easily. "A pet. I'm a person."

"Clumsy when we talk, clumsy when I look at you, clumsy when I challenge you." Maddock marked each point off with a stroke of one finger in the air. "Without even mentioning your unconsciously submissive demeanor. What does that say?"

"I'm a klutz?"

He smiled. "Nice try, but no. It shouts awareness. It says to me you want me to tell you what to do, how and when. The way you look at me, don't look at me and hold yourself. Total sub behavior, pet, kitten, dove, lamb or if you're against animals and birds, little one. Whatever you prefer. All for me."

"Sure of ourselves are we?" Dori said sarcastically. "Never ever lamb. Reminds me of Sunday dinner." Argh, what *was* she saying? "None of them, God do I look like a little one? I am not your sub, or subject or anything, except your PA, even if I'm not the best."

Of course he ignored the sarcasm, but she'd bet he had noted it to be remarked on later.

"You'd better believe it. My sub, no one else's. Now, tomorrow, next week, whenever."

"In your dreams." Dori firmed her lips. Why did she challenge him so much? She liked a good spanking as much as anyone she knew, but for pleasure, not punishment. This contrariness was out of character in the sort of situation she found herself in. Usually she'd send the guy away with a flea in his ear, or be ready to negotiate. So why not with Maddock?

Because it matters. How she recognized that, she had no idea, but the thought that they might play, and then it'd be over would crucify her. She couldn't risk it, surely?

Maddock sighed. "Okay, how about a truce and let's start over."

She let out her breath in one long and noisy exhale. "Sounds good to me."

"Thank the lord for that. Then Dori… Mason… who and what are you?"

Now that wasn't going to be easy. "My name is Dori Mason. I'm weirdly, amongst other things, a stonemason and I, er, make headstones." *And stone overcoats but we won't talk about that. Or the killing part. Not yet if ever.* Damn. All she wanted to do was be open and as ever couldn't. Hell, parts of her life sucked!

Of course he pounced on her choice of words.

"Amongst other things? And those other things would be?"

Oh shit! "Er a crap PA, a lousy cook and a klutz?" *Around you anyway. One Domly look, that I bet you don't even know you are giving, and I'm butterfingers central. And butter.*

Chapter Eight

"The crap PA I'll agree with, the rest I'll reserve judgment." Maddock did his best 'do not fuck with me look', and was pleased to notice Dori jiggle from one foot to the other. Bare feet. With fuck me red nail varnish. It was so at odds with her usual prim and proper appearance it took him aback. Not for long. Her arsy mood seemed to have disappeared as rapidly as it came but he was under no illusion it couldn't reappear as fast if she wanted it to. *Contrariness, thy name is woman.*

She curled her toes under her feet and shifted again. Not only did it show she was uneasy, her tits bounced magnificently under her thin sweater, and he would swear she wore no bra. "Listen, Dori, Mason, whatever you want to call yourself, this is fucking important. Something ugly is in the air and I need to know what it is." Would she understand him, when he didn't really understand himself?

"What's Darke to you?" He'd noticed the frown Darke had given her and it didn't relate to the sort of look you'd give a friend's wife. "And don't say the husband of your mate. That bit I know."

The atmosphere was what you could only call fraught. Dori-Mason whoever she chose to be stared at him, bit her lip, looked at the floor and then at him again. Maddock waited, outwardly patient but inwardly seething and wondering what the hell was going in. He was Darke—and Crabtree's boss—and somehow they were both involved in something he knew nothing about.

The air stirred and Maddock waited for Darke—it had to be him who had entered, since his inner danger radar hadn't set off the itch—to speak.

"Tell him the truth," Darke said wearily. "It

seems we've all been played as fools."

Maddock turned to look at him as he moved towards him and Dori. "By?"

"That's the million dollar question. Crabtree is on his way. He said you'd need to be here."

"Why?" Dori asked in a puzzled voice, as she picked up a glass and twisted it between her fingers. "He's just a carpenter isn't he?" She went red and once more Maddock itched to show her he wasn't *just* a carpenter.

Darke glanced toward Maddock, who nodded, blinked twice in fast succession. Shorthand for 'go ahead'.

"Not exactly," Darke said in a voice devoid of all emotion. Only someone who knew him well, like Maddock did, would detect the tension in his tone. "He's *The* Carpenter."

Dori wrinkled her forehead. "I know he's a carp... oh flying fuckery." The expression sounded strange coming from her. "The... oh God no..." She dropped the glass and once more increased her breakages tally for the day.

Maddock got to the shards before she did. "Do *not* move." The words were clipped and definitely Dom-like. Dori froze with one foot poised to reach the floor within an inch of a particularly vicious-looking splinter. She wobbled and Maddock huffed in exasperation. "Shit, woman, you're a walking disaster area." He picked her up and deposited her on the spanking bench. Sitting upright unfortunately, not as he would prefer her face down and arse in the air. Dori glared and he grit his teeth as he fought his initial impulse. To shake her, kiss her senseless and spank her until she understood what the hell she put him through.

Kiss her senseless? Where the fuck has that come

from?

Dori tugged her top into place and shifted on the bench until her toes touched the floor. That, combined with the amused expression on Darke's face, as he took a dustpan and brush from a cupboard and began to sweep up bits of glass, was the last straw to Maddock.

"What part of do not move, is not comprehensible?" Maddock snapped. "I know you're a shit PA but up until now I did credit you with a modicum of sense. Now, I'm not so sure."

"How *dare* you."

With a reckless disregard toward the broken glass that he'd rebuke her for later, Dori hit the floor with a thump and poked Maddock in the chest. It hardly registered as a touch, but the metaphorical daggers she shot from her eyes hit him harder than any poke or thump could. Apart from furious, she looked…bereft, he decided. Hurt and disillusioned. Why?

"Anyway I'm not your PA anymore," she continued, fiercely. "I quit. You can shove that job up your arse and…"

"Mason," Darke said brusquely. "Remember where you are and who he is. And I don't mean the man who suffered your lack of clerical know-how."

Dori shut her mouth with an audible snap. Maddock replayed that strange exchange and facts began to fall into place. He turned to Darke. "Out. Now."

Darke bowed. "Yes, oh master. With a small 'M'. Don't forget lunch."

He waited until the door closed behind Darke and turned to Dori who stood, arms folded, and leaned against the bench. Everything was falling into place and he was not amused. Not one bit.

"You really are Astrid's friend?" he asked conversationally, once he'd decided Dori was unsettled enough to be off kilter. "Since when?"

"Since almost forever," Dori said indignantly. "Well when we were five or six anyway. I moved when I was eleven but we've stayed friends. Well, there was a glitch when I went to Hong Kong and she went to uni and then got married and divorced and to an ass... oh fuck... Well, he was then anyway."

Maddock grinned. "Yeah, no argument from me there. And how long have you worked for him?"

"Thr...pardon?" She bit her lip.

"Sweetness, enough."

Dori made gagging sounds. "I sound like a syrup pudding. Can't you just call me Mason?"

"God, woman, you're enough to try the patience of a saint, and make me eat a syrup pudding and I hate the stuff. I'm no bloody saint, anything but. So if I say Mason, you'd kneel and submit?" Her eyes widened. "No I thought not. I'm a Master who is at the end of his tether. Plus, it seems I'm your boss. Even if somehow I didn't know it." He ran his hand over his as ever untidy plait. "Look work apart, don't you feel that connection? The, me Tarzan, you Jane thing? As in me Dom you sub? If I think about it, it's been there all along."

He waited with his heart in his mouth. He spoke nothing but the truth, but there was so much more to be said. "Mason, I would like to explore what we could have. What we do have. I'm no sweet talker, but..."

Dori spluttered. "You can say that again. Give me a minute to think." She looked down at her bare feet. "I need to pace."

Maddock took the hint and retrieved the discarded flip flops. "Here." he helped her wriggle her toes through the rubber thongs. "Why don't they fit you?"

"Astrid's," she said briefly. "We usually go

barefoot but parts of the under-floor is being serviced or sommat. So I borrowed these for those areas. Right." She moved so swiftly her skirt brushed against him. "I'm all ears, but can I summarize what I know?"

"Sure." Maddock leaned against a handy cupboard. "Go ahead. I'll say this first that yes, I'm both Crabtree and Darke's boss, which I knew, and yours which, until now I didn't. I did know there was a new Dispatcher but somehow I was told *he* was Mason Dorris. I didn't interfere. Darke is excellent at his job. The Dispatchers is his department. Crabtree was I assumed by his reports all was hunky-dory in London. I've been concentrating on other things." *Specifically who is pretending to be the defunct Department Zee.* That tidbit he kept to himself.

"Ah, yeah well my name is Doris Mason," Dori said. "And I knew the highheidyin was *The* Carpenter, not *a* carpenter."

He loved that slang word for the boss, even if it did give him a mental picture of a guy with a high forehead standing on a plinth.

"Fair enough. And the Dom/sub bit? Are you willing to talk about that when we have time to concentrate on ourselves and describe how we see our lives progressing?" That was the most important thing. Other than who was messing with them of course.

Dori did her agitated hen dance again. Maddock grinned; he was becoming accustomed to it and noticed that as soon as she stopped thinking and just acted, it disappeared. Maybe he needed to give her plenty to do?

"Yes, well hypothetically yes, but not twenty four-seven." She stopped, let her breath out in a long hissing sigh and swallowed. "Plus it has to be said it's been so bloody long since I subbed I'm not sure any of me is fit to do any of it. If you get me."

"I said sub not sex. And there are such things as safe words."

"Oh hell I've put my foot in it again. How mortifying." Every inch of skin that showed was a nice rosy red. "Where's a hole to hide in?"

"Although," he continued as if she hadn't spoken and let his admiring gazes caress her from head to curling toes. "Sex would be good."

Maddock waited until she gave an infinitesimal nod. "But you know what, Mason?" he said conversationally. "Making love would be better still."

Chapter Nine

What a thing to say and expect her to be rational. Every hair on her arms stood on end and her clit tingled. There was no other word for it. *'Sex would be good, making love would be even better…'*

"Oh yes."

"Once we sort out who is fucking with my department and why," Maddock said flatly. "Then we can get on with f…"

"…'ucking each other," she finished with a sense of fatality. Why wasn't she worried? Probably, because it just seemed oh so right. "So what now?"

"Now maybe we do this. Just to see."

Maddock leaned into her and his scents surrounded her. Oh God, why hadn't she realized how much she wanted this man? She opened her mouth and licked her lips.

A klaxon sounded raucous, loud and demanding. Maddock winced and looked around, bemused. "What the hell?"

"Shit, hell, and buggery." Mason grabbed him by the arm. "Come on," she said as she began to pull him toward the door. "That's the red alert. Everyone to the ops room. Something's up. Like a three line whip or whatever you want to call it."

She didn't wait to see if he understood, but once in the corridor, kicked off the flip flops—they just slowed her down—and hitched up her skirts. *"Come on we need to hurry."*

It was a strange situation to be in Mason thought, as Maddock nodded and matched her step for step along the corridor and around a corner. From the opposite direction she could hear the sound of people moving equally as fast.

They collided in front of an open door.

"Down the stairs," Mason said, pleased to see her exercise regime had paid off and she wasn't even breathing heavily. "Along the tunnel and into the ops room."

The guy in front of them turned around and looked at her curiously. Mason remembered she'd never visited whilst anyone was around to see her, except as Astrid's friend.

"Mason," she said briefly and was amused to see his eyes widen. Had there been some stereotyping going on there? She had no time to dwell on the division of the sexes just then. She jumped the last two steps, ran the ten yards to the ops room door, and hurtled in.

Darke stood near a long desk with Crabtree next to him.

Crabtree looked from Mason to Maddock and a faint glimmer of a smile flickered across his features before his normal poker face reappeared. "Sorry to disturb anything important, but I reckoned it had to be me or no one. I think I know something about what's going on."

"Well you're the only one who does," Maddock said as the last few Dispatchers slid across the polished floor and came to a skidding halt. As we all seem to be around?" He glanced at Darke who nodded. "I'll introduce myself and you can fill us in."

Crabtree gave a bark of laughter. "Yeah, it'll be interesting to say the least. Okay, boss, over to you."

"Boss?" Milo said. "You're the bloo... you're The Carpenter? Mad Dog? Shit sorry, but well, fuck me."

"Yes I am and no thanks," Maddock said shortly. God, he hated that sodding nickname. "Call me Maddock or boss. Your choice. I'll answer to either. I assume this is something to do with the attempt to kidnap Astrid and also about Jackson?" he said to Crabtree who inclined his head.

"Got it on one."

"Then we need her and everyone else here."

Darke nodded reluctantly. "I'll ring them."

"No need." Astrid entered along with the other subs/wives/partners and assortment of babies of indeterminate ages. She went across to Crabtree and kissed his cheek affectionately, her animosity toward him Mason was relieved to know, was long gone. "Hi, Dad, causing trouble again?"

Crabtree hugged her. "Not me directly this time, love."

"Hmm, indirectly though. I wonder why I'm not surprised. She handed a baby to him. "Here have a cuddle while we get sorted."

No one gave a hint of amazement at Crabtree being relegated to babysitter.

****

Maddock was amused at how easily the older man held the squirming baby who tried—unsuccessfully—to remove Crabtree's specs.

"No, you monster! They're grandpop's, not yours. Now give over or Mummy won't let me take you to the theme park when you're older. No pirate ships or roller coasters. We don't want that, do we?"

The thought of Crabtree yo-ho-hoing was enough to relieve some of the tension that held Maddock rigid. Beside him Mason hid a grin.

"I'd love to see that," she muttered as Emma and Kirstin, the wives of Milo and Mac followed the other girls into the room with what looked like an overlarge pen of some sort.

"We had to bring the crèche," Emma announced.

"Someone help us fix it, will you, then we can concentrate. I tell you it's darned cumbersome and flipping heavy."

"No sooner said, my sweet." Within minutes the four-sided foam-covered wire enclosure was in the middle of the room and babies crawled around inside.

"Now what?" Astrid sat down on the floor, took up her now grizzling babe from Crabtree, and began to feed her. "Hurry up, it's soon gonna be like painting the Forth Road Bridge, feed-wise."

Crabtree looked toward Maddock who shrugged. "Over to you. I'm clueless here."

"But I sent you an email," Crabtree said. "Day before yesterday, asking for advice. To the office of your carpentry firm like directed. When I didn't get it, I hot footed it up here."

"Ah." Maddock glanced at Mason who went red. "There's been a few problems, office wise lately. Better just tell me what was in it."

Crabtree raised one eyebrow. The room was silent except for a gurgle and a happy, baby-like screech.

"I've found out who Jackson's boss is, was, whatever you want to call it. And why there's so much kerfuffle going on now, even though Jackson is dead and buried. Marcus Verene."

The sound of a chair as it fell over and hit the floor with thump made everyone jump. Except the babies who took it all in their stride.

Maddock turned to look at the dark-haired guy he'd never seen before. "And you are?" he asked in a conversational tone. "Apart from the new boy and I'd bet my pension, the aforementioned late Jackson's boss. Dare I think your name is Marcus Verene?"

The bloke shook his head as all the color leached from his face, and he held onto the wall for support. "Not me. Honestly. I'm Daniel Phillip Traynor. Dan for short. I know him though. His wife was killed a few years back when someone was stopped from bombing part of a university. She was a lecturer and in the wrong place at the wrong time." He sighed heavily. "She was my cousin and pregnant. But I fail to see why that makes him Jackson's boss or what he's got against you all."

"That was one of our first jobs," Maddock said heavily. "We didn't get the info in time and in reality were lucky only one person was killed. What I can't believe is that no one ever made the connection."

"Different names? She never used her married name, ever. They hadn't been married more than a week or so, and it was her first day back at work." Dan sighed. "I expect you'll want to put me under house arrest or something, but I didn't know Marcus was involved with the department. I thought he was a pen pusher in Whitehall."

Darke shot a glance at Maddock who inclined his head. "Do you think you need to be arrested then? There was no reason for you to think he was any different. This is a sideline for him if you like. A get even session. Your choice."

"Then I'll stay, thank you." Dan righted his chair and sat down again.

"So, Lizbeth Rossiter," Maddock mused. "Bugger. And he's waited all this time to get even?"

"No wonder he went for Astrid," Crabtree said. "It was my first job in charge for De... the department. He wouldn't know about you," he said to Maddock. "No one did."

Plus, Maddock thought grimly, he'd not been involved with anyone. He'd had no time.

"I bet when he realized she was Darke's wife he thought he was quids in. Two for one so to speak."

"Okay now we know who and why, what now?" Astrid asked the question on everyone's lips. "Are we in lock down, or do we carry on as normal and hope our defenses work? Because either way we have kids to look after and someone has a dinner to cook."

Chapter Ten

"I think we've got it all covered." Maddock prowled restlessly around the room he'd been allotted, and after dinner dragged Mason into it with him. "What have I forgotten?"

"Nothing, and hell, if you're that worried how come you let Darke make all the arrangements?" Mason asked prosaically. "Everyone knows what to do and how. Everyone is a specialist in what they were allocated, even you, so stop worrying, get some rest and let's be ready when the time comes. You know as well as I do it's not likely to happen in the next hour or so. He can't get within a hundred miles without us knowing. He certainly can't get onto the loch or here without triggering one of the alarms."

He nodded. Of course she was correct, but even so. This wasn't just his life and the lives of his operatives. It was their families as well. Even though all the women knew what went on, and some of them had active roles in the Department, he still couldn't help but be concerned. He decided he better not mention that in front of them if he valued his balls—which he did. "I know, you're right. I just hate this bloody waiting. Waiting and not able to do anything to pass the time."

Mason smiled slowly. The smile of a houri, and mischievous with it. The sort of expression guaranteed to make him wary.

"Oh, I wouldn't say that, *Sir.*" Very gracefully, she slid of the chair she'd been sitting on and knelt in front of him. "I bet my Sir has some ideas."

Maddock stopped dead mid-pace. "Say that again," he demanded, hoarsely. "Just so I can be sure I'm not hearing things."

"I said, Sir, I'm sure you can think of something we can do to pass an hour or two." Mason grinned and dipped her head. "Your pet is ready, my Sir."

Pet? "I thought calling you pet was a big no-go?" Maddock tugged her hair until she looked up at him.

She ran her tongue around her lips slowly, bit the bottom one, and her cheeks reddened. "Ah well, I rather like the sound of it when you say it. Sort of special." Her blush deepened. Just the color he wanted to make her other cheeks.

Maddock considered his options. The room was sparsely furnished. One single bed, a chair, a tiny wardrobe, and an even narrower bedside table with a thin drawer in it. Darke had apologized for the state of it, but half of the rooms were still unusable due to the dodgy heating system. He'd assured the man it was fine but bugger it, now he wished he was anywhere else.

"I haven't got any toys with me," he said as his mind raced. "We'll have to improvise. And we can't do anything deep, if we need to be alert soon." He pulled the chair over to where she knelt and sat down on it. "Over my knee, pet, and make sure your ass is bare for me. A few warm up spanks and a fuck should pass the time?"

Mason looked up and grinned. "Well…" She giggled. "I think that sounds good."

"Safe words." She rattled off the traffic light system, and he grunted. "Then what are you waiting for?"

"Nothing, Sir, except your hand on my ass." Mason lifted her skirt and bunched it around her waist. "I got rid of my undies earlier. Just in case."

He liked her way of thinking. "As long as you remember your body is for me to see and no one else, eh? On to my lap now."

He watched with pleasure as she arranged herself face down, her cunt over his rock hard cock and her ass presented towards him. His palms itched with the need to show her she was his. Such a pity this was short and sweet and not intended to send her into sub space.

"Count to ten, and yes I do just mean ten," he said as she looked up at him in surprise. "Color?"

Mason rolled her eyes. "Green, Sir but, seriously? Only ten? Oops, oh dear, I've questioned your decision. Maybe we need to up it a bit."

Maddock pressed her head down, held her firmly and brought his hand down hard on one luscious ass cheek. It wobbled most satisfactorily and he smiled to himself. "Count, pet." The next spank went onto the other globe, and he rubbed each in turn.

Ten came much too soon, and with a sigh she echoed, he lifted her up and carried her to the edge of the bed." I'm going to enjoy putting my hand print on you so it lasts," he said as he pushed her onto the top of the mattress and she sprawled half on and half off it. Her t-shirt had ridden up and he moved it even higher to show her braless and perfect boobs to him. "Now stay there, do not move, and let me get this hard on out of my jeans and into your sweet cunt. Time's a passing and if I don't come in you I'll…well, fuck knows what I'll do. He fished a condom out of the bedside table drawer and gave thanks to whoever had the foresight to put it in there.

Mason watched with, he hoped, aroused interest as he unzipped his jeans very carefully and released his precum-covered cock. She licked her lips as she stared at it, as if it were the answer to everything she'd ever wondered about, and a lot more besides.

"Hell if you look at me like that I'll come before I get anywhere near you." Maddock shucked his jeans, donned the condom, and took the two steps toward her needed to stand between her legs. "Open wide my love, let me see how wet you are for me."

"Very wet. Needing you now wet." Mason shifted her legs wide and with little finesse he put her feet on his shoulders, and surged into her. The position was awkward, he hadn't even thought of heights, angles, or anything except pushing his dick into her and bringing them both to a climax. On his part that was going to be sooner rather than later. No way would he hold on for long.

Mason's eyes went misty and she mewled as her head thrashed from side to side. He pinched her pert nipples in turn and then put his hand between them to rub the hard nub of her clit.

"Argh… I need." She sobbed the words and it was enough.

"Come for me, love, come for me now."

As she screamed his name and her inner muscles clenched tight around his dick his release flooded trough him. His roar was as loud if not louder than her screams.

God help anyone nearby, if the room wasn't soundproof, they'd be deaf or at least have a severe headache.

****

It was hard not to take deep raspy breaths that made her sound like a thirty-a-day smoker, and even harder to let Maddock withdraw from her. What she really wanted, Mason decided, was a long hard spanking session followed by an even longer bout of lovemaking. *One day.*

Maddock stood up and removed the condom. "Two minutes and we'll head for a shower eh? Let me get rid of this first." He disappeared into the en suite and once she'd heard the toilet flush, Mason struggled to sit up. It might have been short and sweet but by God it had been fast, furious, and fucking amazing. She was enervated, and ready for anything the next few hours threw at them. Once she'd had a shower. Oh she didn't mind the scent of Maddock on her, anything but, but not when the others were around. With a groan as muscles that hadn't been used in such a way for ages protested, she stood up and stretched. Her skirt was creased beyond redemption and her t-shirt stretched in all the wrong places. She looked at herself ruefully. Never mind anyone hearing then, one look at her doing the walk of shame to her room, and they'd all know what she'd been up to.

"I look a mess," she said ruefully as Maddock came back into the room and smiled. He'd dressed in fresh black jeans and a similar colored t-shirt. His hair was speckled with water and his plait very roughly done. "And you look all tidy."

"Shower's ready, and no, you just look very thoroughly loved." He held out his hand and towed her to the bathroom door. Steam rose from the shower stall and she looked at it longingly as Maddock patted her bottom and urged her forward. "In you get. I decided if we showered together we'd never get out. While you're in there I'll get you something to wear. Trousers and top I'd say?"

She nodded. "In my bag. Camo style. Oh and can you bring a sports bra as well, please. These"— she glanced at her boobs, —"Need something to control them if I have to run."

Chapter Eleven

Never in his life had Maddock ever wished he could demand someone be left inside in relative safety. This time he'd have given his eyeteeth to do so. Beside him, concealed in the bushes that surrounded the tiny bay, which after careful deliberation all the Dispatchers decided they thought an intruder would make for, Mason was as silent as him. He glanced at her curiously, her camouflaged face ghostly in the moonlight. Dressed as they were with any skin on show blackened, it was highly unlikely anyone would see them, unless luck was with them and against him and Mason. On a scale of one to ten likelihood, with ten being most probable, he thought it was a big fat zero. They both knew their jobs, even though he admitted he was a bit rusty. Carpentry might use a lot of muscles but not the ones required to sit in a gorse bush and not move for hours. Okay, it had been less than twenty minutes, but it seemed like hours. Lord, he felt like the new boy, not the boss.

Ever since they had left the building he sensed the determination in his companion. A focus equal to his. Mason spoke softly in his ear. The pitch was perfect. One nobody more than a few inches away would be able to hear.

"ETA three minutes." She had the wires connecting them to Milo and the sensors he watched from the ops room. He had, Milo said bitterly, drawn the short straw. As several of the others nodded and grinned, Maddock guessed it was a well-known gripe, especially as Milo was one of the acknowledged experts in that particular field.

He'd glanced at Maddock who shrugged. "Win some, lose some." Maddock had made certain no one suspected him of not having every faith in them. He did and he was content to let this be Darke and the Dispatchers show, not his. He was, if not happy, resigned to being a dogsbody.

Someone had to be.

"Coming here?" he asked. "Any numbers?"

She moved her shoulders carefully. "Nope. I think it's just one though, from the description of the vessel, and oh boy here he is. Not very careful eh? He's making enough noise for a troupe of cheerleaders when their team needs a rallying cry. Stupid asshole. He deserves all he gets."

That picture she conjured up was enough to make Maddock stifle a chuckle. She did have a way with words.

The splashing of a paddle grew louder. When the canoe slid into the bay, shiny in the moonlight, she nodded to the beach. "Let him land and we'll follow him. Darke will want a word or ten I reckon. Then it'll be up to, I dunno you or whoever to decide what happens next."

Maddock was certain it wasn't going to be up to him unless he was asked, and knowing Darke as he did, was reasonably sure the request wouldn't be made. It was Darke's job. This island was his to run as he thought fit. Maddock had no intention of interfering. He waited alongside Mason, while a remarkably thin man, dressed in—holy hell a green balaclava and what looked like a Dalmatian patterned onesie—got out, splashed in the shallows and drew the canoe onto the shingle. Noisily.

"You'd almost think he wants to be seen and heard," Mason spoke in an undertone, "This smells."

So did she, deliciously. Not the time, nor the place. Later, he promised himself. Later he'd have that scent in his nostrils as well as the scent of sex.

The man looked around and inexpertly tied the canoe's painter to a gorse bush. One breath of wind and it would come free and he'd lose his mode of transport. Not that it would matter. It was highly unlikely he'd be leaving in it. Not alive anyway.

Noiselessly they followed the man up the winding track towards the house as it skirted gorse bushes and trees. Although the sensors along the way worked, the trip wires had been removed. They wanted to see what he was up to before they apprehended him. The guy made no attempt to hide himself or aim for stealth, as he crunched noisily over patches of strategically placed gravel. Maddock glanced at Mason who shrugged. She was as much at a loss as he was.

As the man approached the edge of the woods, he hesitated for the first time. Then he slowly removed his balaclava and shook his head. Long reddish blond hair spilled over his shoulders and down his back. The moon outlined the body with all its curves.

"Fucking hell, it's a bloody girl."

Nothing like stating the obvious. Mason nodded. "What now? Take her?"

"Wait a sec. What's she doing?"

As they watched from the edge of the woods the girl took off the onesie, which Maddock noticed was actually a patterned boiler suit, the sort of thing that had been in fashion a few years before, albeit, briefly. She rolled her shoulder before she straightened her back and walked purposefully towards the house.

"A decoy?" Maddock asked doubtfully. It seemed somewhat farfetched that anyone would send a slip of a thing to the island. Not only did it have enough keep out government property notices to keep a sign writer occupied for a year, it only had a very few places to safely land.

"Milo says not. Darke says we follow and assess. He also told me that you're the one with all the knowledge we'll need about anything."

He liked Darke's support even though at that moment Maddock considered it misplaced. He needed to hone up a lot of skills. "Doubtful, and anyway in this you're the boss. I'm rusty in the field. On three?"

"Yeh. Right, one, two…three." Maddock followed Mason across the lawn and pondered on how this crazy weekend would finish. It had been surreal to say the least, and now here he was taking orders from someone under him.

That expression made him chuckle silently. Not always workwise either. Ahead of them the girl headed straight towards the main building.

"At least she's not going to the block," Mason said softly. "But this is seriously screwy. "What do you reckon? Take her now?"

"Hold on." Maddock considered. "No, let her go in. Milo will have her covered and I'm guessing there's no more unwanted or uninvited visitors in the vicinity. Let's see what happens."

"Fair enough. Nothing's been reported."

The intruder, if that was what you would call her, walked up to the large wooden door and hammered on it. The thumps reverberated back to where Maddock and Mason stood. He raised his eyebrow in query. Mason shrugged. "No idea but I reckon we can go in with her." She set off at a brisk pace and Maddock followed. By the entrance the girl still beat on the door with both fists. Then she leaned on it. It opened just as Maddock and Mason got to with a couple of yards and the girl almost fell inside.

"That's a nice way to be greeted. I love me a girl on her knees." The tall dark-haired man who had opened the door nudged her with his toes. "I think you better come in and greet everyone else in a more conventional way. Well," Dan guffawed. "Conventional to most people. Here we prefer the sub on knees greeting."

"You? What the fuck are you doing here?" The girl poked him in the chest.

Dan's eyes narrowed. "Enough, sweetness. Watch what you are saying or are you fond of a mouth washed out with soap?"

"Hell on wheels, have I had some weird and wonderful potion for my dinner? Making me hallucinate and see nasties?" She scrambled to her feet, ignored Dan's comments and fisted her hands into tight balls. "What have you done with my brother?"

Maddock took the three steps necessary to really see the girl's face. Up close the green flecks in her otherwise brown eyes were pronounced and reminded him of someone. She appeared ready to do a serious injury to anyone who got in her way. "Answer me, you bastard."

"Who the hell is your brother?" Maddock asked as Dan grabbed hold of the girl's hands and held them high enough for her to have to stand on tiptoe. *Come on, who the fuck does she look like?*

"The cops know I'm here." She spat out the words and stared around at them all. "Scaredy cats come in numbers do they?"

"Bullshit about the cops. Why would they?" Maddock had to admire her spirit even if not her intentions, or her sanity in goading them, especially Dan, who looked fit to murder someone.

"I left a note with a friend. I don't trust it when people aren't open."

The girl glared at him and Mason took a step to stand next to him. Goodness knows what she thought was about to happen.

"Your brother, sweetness," Dan said. "The boss man is waiting. He's a bit like me. Not a patient person. I might know him and you. He doesn't."

"What?" The girl turned around and really looked at Maddock and Mason as if she'd only just noticed them, which would be a lie. She'd been aware of who was where all the time. She wiped her hands on her jeans and Maddock knew.

"Marcus Verene," Dan said before anyone else could. "Shall I spill the beans and say you're Rhonda?"

Dan does know her. There's a story there for later.

"Yes, you know that, but…" She spat out the words and then looked bewildered. "Where is he? The last I heard was he was doing marine biology for the government or something around here. No one's heard of him but I saw *him*." She gestured toward Mac who along with his lady Kirstin appeared along the corridor. "I've seen him before so I asked someone who he was. The woman in the post office was most chatty. Said you worked for the government and lived on here. So." She shrugged. Here I am and where's Marcus? He's all I've got now." Her eyes were bleak.

"That's what we'd all like to know," Maddock said. "Because he sure as hell isn't here."

"No? Then where is he? I thought he"— she stared at Dan again —"would help, but I should have known better."

Dan put his hands in the air. "Hey, bugger all to do with me, sweetness. You left."

Rhonda looked at them all wildly and burst into tears. "Shit, I hate being a watering pot, but I need to see him."

"Don't we all." Crabtree appeared like a genie out

of a bottle. "Why do you specifically?"

"I'm pregnant."

"You bloody what?" Dan's voice raised several notches before he took a deep breath and shook his head. "Not likely, sweetness."

"If you say so. Anyway I don't care what you say. Where's Marcus? He'll help me." Her eyes filled with tears. "Oh shit I didn't mean to say that. I don't need him because I'm up the duff. I need him for something else. I'm confused."

"Now I wonder why?" Dan said flatly. "That's a new phenomenon." He turned on his heel and walked back towards the ops room.

"Ah...er..." Crabtree faltered and glanced around in panic. "Perhaps um..."

Maddock looked toward Darke who shrugged helplessly. No help there. Mason and Astrid stepped forward.

"C'mon, you come with us and calm down, then we can all try and sort out what the hell is happening." Astrid cuddled Rhonda. "Does the papa know?"

Rhonda sighed. "He does now."

Chapter Twelve

"Can I say shit?" Mason walked back into the ops room and headed for Maddock. He put his arm around her and nuzzled the top of her head, heedless of who saw. "All okay?"

Mason shook her head. "Not exactly. It sounds bloody complicated if you ask me. By the way, Dan. You're needed in the small sitting room."

"One sec, Dan," Maddock said. "Any clues as to where bloody Marcus Verene is?"

Dan stood up. "I reckon long gone. He's a shit. Rhonda has never really asked for his help and now she has the fucker had ignored her."

He closed his eyes and when he opened them, Mason decided she'd never experienced the degree of anguish she saw there. She took a step forward and stopped. This wasn't her job to dictate. Instead she stirred restlessly. Maddock squeezed her shoulder and she sighed. "Whatever, Dan, you're needed."

"Best go," Darke said. "There's nothing else we can do except be on our guard. "Keep your walkie talkie handy."

Dan nodded. "I'm rostered on duty anyway, so I won't be long."

"Nope, you've been swapped. As of now. You'll be more use elsewhere." Darke didn't spell out where. There was no need.

Once Dan left the room, Darke pushed himself off from where he'd been leaning on the edge of the desk. "Bossman, over to you."

Maddock looked around the room in an exaggerated fashion. "Who? Oh me… Hell, this is your play. However, if you want my not so valuable input, I'd say no one is going to arrive here without our knowledge and I suggest we all get some sleep in the usual rostered fashion. Tomorrow we think again. I doubt it's going to go away."

"Not until he gets to one of us," Crabtree said. "I'll do tonight, instead of Dan, with whoever else is on if that's okay with my bosses?"

"Hell yeah." Darke and Maddock both spoke at once. "You're on with Milo. He'll be back in a minute. He's doing the first security checks."

"Fair enough." Crabtree switched the coffee maker on and the gorgeous aroma of Kenyan roast filled the room. Maddock's tummy rumbled. They never had gotten around to post-dinner coffee.

"You lot go and see your ladies. As I haven't got one to see I'm happy to be one of the night watchmen."

Maddock sketched a wave around the room. "Reconvene at seven if we're not called out." He took Mason's arm and began to propel her toward the door. "Night all." When they were in the corridor he turned to her. "Where's the nearest food?"

She remembered the words he'd whispered to her in the middle of lovemaking and laughed. "According to you earlier, here." She patted her boobs and jiggled them.

"To enjoy feasting on delectable offerings, those my love, I need sustenance of a different kind first. A curry would be perfect," he added wistfully. "A roast and trimmings even better."

"At this time of night you'd end up with gut ache," she replied. "And not manage anything else. How about homemade soup? Thick and full of veg."

His tummy rumbled again. "I guess that's a yes, please."

Within five minutes Mason ladled gently steaming and incredibly aromatic soup into two bowls and handed one to him. Half an hour later they were in the room allocated to him because, she said with a twinkle, she'd given hers to Rhonda. "I hope you don't mind. I could bunk in the lounge if you'd prefer?" she added demurely. "I'd hate to cheat you out of your bed."

The gleam in his eyes showed he was happy with that. "I'd hate it even more to be cheated out of my dessert," Maddock said. "I left space for a delicious handful of body you know."

"Really?" He'd eaten two bowls of soup and several slices of bread. "I hope you don't get indigestion."

"This food is perfect to aid my digestion, not upset it," Maddock replied gravely and then spun her around in a circle.

The room blurred as her feet left the ground. "Maddock you nut, I'll go all giddy and not be able to ravish you." Mason buried her head in his neck, and shut her eyes. She hated things that spun around. Of course he didn't know that. It wasn't something that had come up in the 'where the hell have you put the Johnstone bill' conversations they'd had. As the room slowed Mason had a brief flash of guilt. "I'm sorry I was such a shit PA. But I had to make sure you didn't really get to know me and wonder why I was there."

She hoped he would take the bait. It was time to own up to the last bit of the subterfuge.

He did. "Ah yes, My PA." Maddock slid her down his body. Every inch of her front moved oh so slowly over his erect cock. Red hot arousal shot through her as her mouth went dry, her sight blurry and her clit achingly hard. Her skin tingled and pain of the best kind hit her as Mason dropped her onto the bed, lifted her top with one hand and drew her boob into his mouth with the other. And bit her nipple.

She arched up off the mattress with a moan as he covered her face with the soft cloth of her top. Her arms were lifted and her hands wrapped around the top of the headboard.

"Do not move." Maddock the Master was back in full force.

Her, "No, Sir," was an automatic response. His chuckle reached her even though it was muffled by material.

"Good girl. I think we need to talk and then maybe play or punish. I wonder which. First things first, though. You were going to tell me about my totally incompetent but always around PA." The mattress depressed as she assumed he sat on it, then a typical Scottish chill wafted over her pussy as presumably her skirts were gathered around her waist. His finger circled her clit. Mason hoped it was his, she didn't fancy a threesome or going public.

"It's ah…" Damn, she couldn't concentrate as he played with her clit and almost lazily put one finger inside her.

"Ah?" A second finger followed the first. "Ah what?"

"Ah well I'm not usually as klutzy, but I got even more flustered around you than I had to and couldn't help it," she said in a rush.

"And the rest."

Both fingers were withdrawn and she felt bereft. Empty and… *shit what did he say?* "Oh Darke asked me to keep an eye on you. You'll have to ask him why, specifically. All I got told was someone might try to eliminate you, and he really didn't want it to happen. That was all." She held her breath. It was true but by God it sounded pathetic.

"Hmm, sounds like Darke to keep us both in the

Dark. I just wondered what the hell I'd done to deserve you. Now I know. You were meant for me. Just not as my PA."

A shrill bell sounded and she began to wriggle off the bed. A large hand held her in place.

"Did I say you could move?"

"Well no but. But." The bell shrilled on.

The hand that held her moved and smacked her pussy. She had the irreverent thought that she'd given the hand a mind and a will of its own, before she replied. "No Sir."

"Exactly. Now stay there while I answer it."

Try as she might she couldn't fathom out more than the odd 'yeah, good true, right, eight. Bye', before there was silence. Mason held her breath as the air moved.

"Now where were we?" Maddock asked.

"You were going to tell me what that was all about maybe, Sir?"

He chuckled. "I'd like to spank you for your sass and keep you in the dark as Darke did to us, but I won't. It was Milo. Verene is in Thailand. All alerts off. For now. So, let me decide. Ah yes. As I said before, pet. Do not move."

"Yes, Sir. Or should that be no, Sir? Anyway I'll do as you say, Sir."

"Good girl." She lay there in the semidarkness and wondered if it was pleasure or punishment she deserved. Then she found out.

"I want to create our pattern in wax on you, pet. May I?"

Behind the cloth she blinked. "Yes, Sir." Her pussy clenched and her juices gathered. Our pattern? She savored those words, they sounded perfect.

"Then let's get you naked and onto a towel. Let

go of the rails."

Her jumper was pulled over her head and she blinked in the candlelit room. He'd been busy. Candles dotted almost every flat surface and created an erotic and romantic space. Mason lifted her ass as Maddock tugged down her skirt and spread a linen towel under her. Then with a glint in his eyes she'd never seen before he put her hands back around the headboard. "Do I need to tie you, or will you stay like that?"

"No need to tie them, Sir." She'd do as he asked. "Well, I'm not sure about my feet," she added honestly. "If it hurts before it morphs into a sweet pain I might try to curl up."

He grinned, and pulled a pair of individual ankle cuffs with ties to them out of his pocket. "Spread them, pet."

It was fascinating to watch how he prepared. Mason stayed as he directed and did her best to quell the silly frisson of fear that hit her. She'd never tried wax play and it was one thing she often thought about. And it was Maddock for heaven's sake. Maddock, not any old Dom.

"Color, pet?" Maddock stood next to her, a candle in each hand.

"Green, Sir."

"Then my love let's play. I warn you, this will be hot."

He wasn't wrong. That first drop of wax on her tummy made her bite her lip; the second clench the rails so hard she'd have bruises. The sting followed by brief red-hot pain and the sense of something hard on her skin was new and at times disconcerting.

After each carefully placed drop of wax, Maddock waited until she assured him she was green. Then all of a sudden the sensation chanced from hot and sore to hot and arousing. She began to float.

"That's my good girl. Shall I take a photo to show you? You're in that oh so sweet sub space now aren't you?" Somehow she managed to answer both questions in the affirmative before she let go and let the gorgeous floating sensation claim her totally.

When eventually she came down to earth, she was wrapped in a soft blanket in Maddock's arms. He smiled down at her and kissed the tip of her nose. "Okay?"

She nodded. "More than."

"You need chocolate and water. Both here."

Mason drank and ate when he held the water bottle and the chocolate bar to her mouth. Then she looked down at her tummy and breasts. "Where's the wax?"

Maddock passed her his phone with a picture pulled up on the screen. "That's how it looked. You're not ready for it to be left on yet."

I will be soon. Mason looked at the picture and laughed. It was beautifully done. Very artistically placed wax over her front in intricate whorls and cobwebby patterns. But the script on her tummy made her giggle. 'From PA to pet.'

"That's me."

"And pet to collared sub, and then wife one day?" Maddock asked carefully. "When you're ready."

Her heart missed a beat. Even though the words were said casually, the look in his eyes was intent.

Mason scrambled off the bed and knelt on the floor next to it. "In a heartbeat, My Sir. Whenever you want."

Epilogue

The Dispatchers and their partners sat around the comfortable room they used for general briefings. Chairs, settees, even a beanbag was occupied. Sadly none of the occupiers looked happy. Why would they be pleased with a demand to meet at six am? Maddock understood. He sure as hell wouldn't have been either, except needs must.

Milo sprawled on the beanbag and grunted. "Crap seat." He shuffled and the beanbag made its usual scrunching noise and the contents shifted under the blue striped canvas cover. He raised his eyebrows as his lady glared at him. "Well it is. Those fuckers got in before me and copped the sensible ones. This one makes me think of labor."

"Suck it up sweetie," she said gently, as a snigger went around the room and thankfully lowered the tension that reverberated through everyone. "Be happy you'll never need it to go through labor, and let's kick the asses that need kicking."

Maddock grinned and then forgot them. Other things needed to be addressed and sadly he was about to up that tension again. He coughed theatrically to gain people's attention and waited until everyone seemed settled, glanced around the room, with its comfy oversized chairs and pretty decorations, and breathed deeply. This wasn't going to be easy, or pleasant. Maddock knew why he was like a cat on a hot tin roof and wished to hell he wasn't.

Scary times.

The room reeked relaxation. Even the rugs and throws complimented the plain grey walls. It was a room to forget the cares and worries of their lives in. A tiny fridge stocked with anything anyone could want and the microwave ready to nuke a curry stood on a long counter, at one end and a TV at the other. Now it was time to upset the ambiance.

Breathe, deep breaths. Calm down. Sadly, try as he might, his silent instructions to himself didn't work, not at that moment. Not with the inhabitants who lounged, stood rigid, or who wondered what the fuck. This meeting had been called as Maddock had said, not as a normal briefing. It was an extraordinary general meeting. And not all of the Dispatchers were there.

Therefore, it would be more truthful to say most of the Dispatchers and partners were in attendance. Maddock smiled briefly at Mason who watched with interest as he glanced from one person to another and waited until Darke nodded to him.

"Only Dan and Rhonda missing. I suggested they had a private heart-to-heart."

Maddock sat down next to Mason and stretched out his long legs. Maybe it would be easier to do this in a less 'me boss, you minions' way? Mason leaned into him, and he was grateful for her presence, even if the information he was about to impart would hit her hard. He prayed it wouldn't fuck up their relationship. Strange how someone became so important in such a short time.

"It's up to them to sort their private lives out. We need to do the rest. I asked everyone to come because what's happened here in the past will affect all our futures."

Beside him, Mason stirred uneasily. Tension radiated from her and hit him like a body blow. Outwardly she seemed so calm and collected but he knew better. Evidently she understood something big was going to happen, and he was bloody certain that by now her 'be aware' itch was dashing up and down her spine so hard she was damned sure she wasn't going to like whatever it was.

Maddock stood up—*shit I'm like a jack in the box*—and began to pace. Everyone turned their heads to follow his path across the room and back again.

"Bossman you're making me giddy," Darke said. "Spit it out for fuck's sake. Who do we need to kill, how, where, when and why?"

"Who?" Maddock stopped his pacing and swung around to lean on the windowsill and look at glance around them all. "Why, no one. The Dispatchers are being disbanded. Therefore, never, nowhere, and no reason. Tomorrow we begin anew."

The silence in the room was absolute.

The End

KERA FAIRE

DEDICATION

To Rhonda. This is for you. I promised you a Dark Isle story and I hope you like it.

AUTHOR'S NOTE

For those of you who follow the series, this story starts several months before The Carpenter, and ends after The Carpenter ended.
Kera

KERA FAIRE

THE CLEANER

Death Isle, 7

Kera Faire

Copyright © 2017

Chapter One

Near London, England

Blue, Rhonda decided, was her most hated color. Firstly, due to the blue uniform of the copper who stopped her for speeding, and then gave her a lecture for driving at 42 in a 40 limit. What a wanker. He was more interested in her boobs than her driving. She gave him her best 'fuck you' stare and eventually he gave her a lecture—and his phone number—not a ticket. She forgot the lecture and threw his number in the bin.

Then the blue nail varnish she spilled on her newly washed floor. After that the blue paint on a shop doorway she didn't notice until it was too late. Her lovely white jeans were now blue striped. Lastly this bloody blue line that gave her the information she didn't want.

Pregnant. The rabbit died.

Up the duff. Bun in the oven, knocked up and in the pudding club. The family way beckoned. Take your pick. Whatever euphemism you used it all added up to the same thing. In seven months give or take—after all she couldn't be sure of the conception date—she'd be in agony. Plus, no doubt, cussing hot as hell, panty-dropping men. The thought of a bloke in Barbie pink, or little mermaid panties conjured up some mind-boggling pictures. *Oh good grief, now I'm adding overactive hormones to the mix.*

Don't lie about the date I know to the bloody minute... No doubt she would also be swearing to castrate any virile male who came within fifty yards of her. Wasn't that what everyone said? Swear never again and twelve months later...Not her. She'd actually swear to the castration now, let alone later.

Damn droopy condoms, dodgy seafood, virile men and fertile women.

Why oh why had she jumped head—okay pussy—first into a relationship with a guy in the services of all things, who told her he was only going to be around for a few months before he was posted overseas?

Because I'm an idiot and thought with my clit and not my brain. And I was ready for sex. Good sex, and boy was it good. Not just the sex, but all the trimmings that went along with it. Now though it seemed someone, somewhere, was having the last laugh. Because that 'no ties except around your hands and feet, sweetness,' had come back to bite her on the bum.

And not the bite of a flogger or her Sir, either. No, 'sweetness, present for me'. No, 'what a good girl my pet is'. No 'don't come until I say so'. No traffic light safe words if she wasn't happy. This was in your face 'grow up and decide what next' time. She wasn't going to be able to cry 'yellow I need to think about this'. This was full on green: it's happening.

Think dammit. Deal with it like an adult. With one last glare at the offending line, she found some paper and a pen. She always thought better when she had a plan.

Find out for sure if that blue line is right. After all, didn't they say it could be wrong? Whoever the mysterious "they" were. The pang that she might not be expecting hit her so hard she dropped the pen. She didn't want to be pregnant, did she? Not 'single, no father around and no support' pregnant?

"Find out." She dialed the doctor's surgery to make an appointment before she could change her mind.

"You're in luck, I've had a last minute cancellation. Get here by half past and you're in, Rhon." Sandy, the practice manager, was a friend from nursery school days. They'd attended the tiny village school together, taken the bus to the senior school ten miles away, drooled after the same blokes, and ended up at the same university, although taking different courses. Sandy had gone for business and management and Rhonda, linguistics. They'd both ended up in Strathcardle without knowing the other would be there.

As far as Rhonda was concerned it was serendipity, and as at that moment not much else was, she'd be glad of it.

"Around eight weeks as a rough guess," the doctor, a middle-aged cheerful woman said, as she filled a prescription for iron. "And you're as healthy as you should be. Does that mesh?"

Rhonda nodded. "Yeah, it does, thanks." Evidently it had all happened the last time she'd met him. They'd been at it like rampant rabbits on speed, before he'd done his, 'it was great, loved every minute, and sadly I've got to go' act. That was the time he'd asked her if they should keep in touch, and she was so pissed at his seemingly casual farewell she'd said no. It was good while it lasted but now it was over.

He, sod it, accepted it without any show of regret, and didn't leave a forwarding address. Even his phone just rang out 'unobtainable' when she tried to contact him that way. She'd deleted the number then, and tried to think good riddance. So what if she thought she knew it off by heart, it wasn't answered. It was now number non grata or whatever. So he needn't say she hadn't tried to give him the good—or bad—news that he was going to be a dad.

You can't try; you deleted it. Rhonda ignored that tiny nagging voice. Here she was, she thought: up the duff and no way of saying, 'oh by the way, the present you left me will arrive in about seven months give or take.' Even less time to get into gear for a new life.

Liar, liar, pants on fire, you do know it. Maybe so, but she wasn't going to acknowledge it...or was she? *Grow up, grow a pair and bloody ring it, just in case there is someone on the other end.* Her heart beat too fast as she pressed the keys and waited. Then she didn't know whether to laugh or cry as she heard the tinny voice telling her he wasn't there and 'Please leave a message after the tone...'

What the hell should she say? In the end she blurted it out. "Hi this is Rhonda, if you get this I've got some important news you need to know." Anything else? No, if he was interested he'd ring back.

He didn't.

Damn him, she'd go to cry—or not—on her brother's shoulder. Rhonda didn't expect Marcus, her older and she admitted, wiser, sibling to solve anything, just hear her out. Agree with her decision and if nothing else, root for her and buy her bananas or whatever she craved. Marcus and she always stood by each other, come what may. After his wife had died—killed in a senseless act of terrorism—he'd become harder, less approachable. Less willing to see two sides of anything, and it was his way or no way. However, not when it concerned Rhonda, she hoped. Although she generally took care not to bother him, he would come through for her, she was sure. The only problem was finding him.

"So, do I go ahead and sort out antenatal appointments or...?" the doctor said in a tactful voice, bringing her back to the there and now. "There's time yet for you to decide what you think is best. I can set up an appointment for you to discuss every option."

What? An appoint... oh no, not in a million years. That broke into her reverie about burning oil for men with overactive cocks and marching on the condom factory demanding they sorted their elasticity problem out. "Dec...Oh I've decided. I'm not having a termination," Rhonda said firmly. She made her mind up about that as soon as the doctor said those two words 'eight weeks'. "Hit me with the list of do's and don'ts, and I'll go to the health food shop on the way home."

"Have some leaflets and make your next appointment with Sandy," the doctor said with a laugh. "You're hale and hearty, in good health, so no need to go overboard. Just think before you eat and I'll see you soon."

Rhonda nodded and stood up. There *was* a lot to think about, and not just food.

She started some of that thinking half an hour later as she stood in her kitchen with a decaf coffee and a homemade bun. She stared at the bun, and had to giggle. A bun in the oven took on a whole new meaning now. Very slowly she picked out a currant and gazed at it thoughtfully before she put it into her mouth. He'd loved currants and had even persuaded her to make him garibaldis, those flat biscuits he jokingly called squashed flies. Rhonda put the bun down in a hurry, and picked up a lemon one. No way was she going to give her child any reason to *want* to eat squashed flies.

She sipped the coffee and contemplated her still flat tummy. How long before she had to do up her jeans with a safety pin or elastic between the button and hole? What she understood about pregnancy could be written on a pinhead. 'Feel sick, get a bulge'. Was it shameful she was clueless about all things antenatal, apart from, she thought, no alcohol in pregnancy. That would be fine, baby first and, as two small glasses got her squiffy, it was no chore to drink soda water instead.

See 'clueless'. The first thing on her agenda was to read the leaflets, and maybe buy a book—— Pregnancy for the uninitiated—or something. Then, play 'hunt the Marcus'.

What about hunt the papa-to-be? Sod that thought. Go away. Rhonda finished the coffee, made a note to only buy decaf in future, ate a salad, and opened her laptop.

Five hours later she had accomplished some of her self imposed tasks and not others. She'd confused herself even more over what was good and what was not for her over the next seven or so months. She read up on breastfeeding, and fixed bits of the information in her mind. Stay clear of liver and soft cheese, both of which she hated anyway, so that was not a problem, but weaning and god help her, the terrible twos, sounded daunting. Somewhat defiantly ignoring all the old wives' tales, she ordered enough pregnancy books to open a bookshop, and succumbed to two tiny baby vests. Sod those who said it was bad luck—and marked out the 'Blooming Bumps' web site for the not-too-distant future. Some of the dresses on there were amazing. Not that she was much of a dress girl, but then maybe she'd prefer them rather than things around her waist? Would she even know where her waist was? It was a journey into the unknown, that was for sure.

For the umpteenth time, Rhonda checked her phone. No text, no email, no WhatsApp from her brother or her ex. Nothing. Now what? The father-to-be was god knows where, and it seemed so was her brother.

Gloomy and fed up, not at all like her normal upbeat self, she wandered into the jungle, also known as her garden, and stared at a clump of bamboo. What should she do? She hadn't been sick—yet. Her appetite for food hadn't diminished, although with hindsight, she had found her tastes had altered a bit. After all, she'd never really been into piccalilli, and now she craved it. And eaten more apples and less grapes. Was that due to pregnancy or the fact the grapes were not at their best? Heaven knew, she didn't.

Work was no problem; her job as a virtual PA to a local joinery firm could be done anywhere with Internet access. Her home, apart from the garden, was easily managed and could be left, as long as her neighbors knew she was away and went in periodically to move any post she received and twitch curtains. All of which would be fine and dandy if she had an idea where to go. She mooched back into the kitchen and stared at the postcard she'd stuck onto the fridge. A picture of a loch, and...

"You twerp. What a numpty." Rhonda took it down carefully and turned it over. The postmark was indecipherable, but the words written by her brother weren't.

"Lovely area, going to enjoy the aquatic biology here, even if it's not the sea. Island hopping takes on a whole new meaning on the lochs. Be good and I owe you a curry."

It would be a while, she decided, before she'd fancy the curry. How on earth, though, had she forgotten the card that had arrived a few weeks earlier? Not that it said much, but the picture was of Loch Lomond, taken (it said) from somewhere called Balmaha. Surely that would be a good place to start?

Time to make another list.

****

He was so good at making her want more.

How could she have ever sent him away? He was the only person who could make her feel like this—alive, ready to do whatever her Sir told her. To wait, patiently—almost—as he gave her the attention she required and allowed and encouraged her to fly and sink into that perfect sub space of knowing she was his. Rhonda moaned as her ass warmed and her breathing sped up. It was a dream, surely? Nothing as good as this sense of belonging had been hers since he went. But it seemed oh so real. It *had* to be real.

He'd come back. Joy filled her along with arousal. Her thighs were damp and her clit hard. The pulse between her pussy and ass throbbed as she waited for what might, just *might* happen next.

"Hello, my sweetness. Is my pet ready for me?"

"Yes, Sir. Oh yes."

The heat and the intensity of his gaze as he stroked her cheek, the way his eyes sparkled and his lips quirked, were enough for her nipples to become hard stinging nubs. His cock—oh my his magnificent cock—the tip shining with the evidence of his arousal, made her throat dry and her body tingle. He bent and took one of those hard nubs into his mouth with a nip and a bite at the same time as his dick pressed against her pussy. Rhonda moved restlessly, inched nearer and gave into one long, breathy moan of need. She was eager to taste him, experience him inside her once more and relieve the heightening tension and arousal that flooded through her body.

"Enough, sweetness. I say when, do I not?" He

pinched her non-bitten nipple. "Your arousal is mine to give or deny. Be a good little pet and all will be yours."

That sharp instantaneous pain made her jump, even as he spread her legs and positioned his cock at her entrance.

"Ready? I'm going to ride you hard and fast. Hear you scream my name and 'thank your Sir'. For we both need this don't we, pet? Get ready and ..."

"No..." Her scream echoed around the room. "God, no, the baby, n..." She opened her eyes.

Her ass hurt for all the wrong reasons.

It was a bloody dream.

She'd fallen asleep sitting at the table and half slipped off the bench. So one cheek was on cushion and one on wood and the crack of her ass was wedged most uncomfortably between the two.

Chapter Two

A month or so later
Scotland

Dan worked smoothly and efficiently. This time of the night, or to be precise, the very early morning, was his favorite. Darkness was his friend. Here he could clean up and apart from the pigs no one would bother him. As they were fed, watered and satisfied, they snuffled and almost treated him as a friend. Not that he thought it would be so if they were hungry. He'd seen how they devoured their meat, be it animal, mineral, or vegetable. He spotted one human tooth, and used a shovel to take it out of the sty, and put it into storage. It would be sent away later, as all molars were, to be made into a necklace. That thought made him grin. How many tourists in Papua New Guinea or Greece really knew what their super duper hippy necklaces were made of? Did they realize their so-called plastic wasn't?

He was in accord with Mac and Milo though; the hogs seemed to prefer human flesh. They weren't fussy if it were dead or alive, but got arsy—or should that be hoggy—if it had been frozen and not defrosted properly. He whistled under his breath as he scoured the area from the main landing site to the pigsty and on to the house. Nothing should be amiss; they were all too fucking good at their jobs to make mistakes. But it was common sense, not to say standard procedure, for someone to do a final sweep—with night glasses if necessary—after the checks. Tonight it was his turn to make sure all was safe and well.

Apart from Mac's snares and cameras. He still hadn't been given the secrets to them.

Soon, though.

If he had his way, Dan would cheerfully work every night. Since his last, sadly fucked up relationship ended—when an urgent phone call hauled him back to London and eventually here, to Scotland—and he'd had to say 'thanks for everything I'm off', he'd been pussy-less. And looked to be staying that way for the foreseeable future.

His lady, his sweetness, his pet, wasn't likely to forgive him any time soon. *If only* she even deigned to see him. *If only* he ever got the time to find her. *If only* she would listen. Those bloody two words again. *If only.* As his late Granny Soutar used to say, 'Ach, *if* and *only* are the twae most awfy sad words in the world, bairn. Dinnae use them.' As none of those scenarios were likely at that moment in time, Dan was resigned to staying celibate unless he used the services of Pam and her five sisters—his palm and fingers. And as that alternative didn't appeal to him, he'd stay unsatisfied and horny as hell.

The area was clean, and Dan thumbed the information via his phone to Darke, who was—as far as he knew—in the control room, and no doubt warm, dry—as ever it had started to rain—and waiting to hear from Dan.

He was, he acknowledged, very much the newbie on the island. When the idea was mooted that perhaps his specific talents could be honed on Dark Isle, known 'in the trade' as 'Death Isle', Dan wasn't sure. He enjoyed what he already did. Making sure a certain type of operations undertaken by those in the government's employ were completed tidily. Specifically those whose job descriptions were intentionally vague, and who were not generally named. He'd said so in no uncertain terms.

Until the magic words, 'The Dispatchers' were

mentioned. Then he jumped at the chance, did his initial extra training all over the place, hence his 'Dear Joan' session with his lady, and a few weeks ago ended up on Dark Isle.

Where he discovered the midges were buggers who got everywhere, it rained a lot, which helped keep the bastards at bay for a while, and when the sun shone it was one of the most beautiful places in the world—except for the midges. If they weren't there, it was paradise. Sadly those latter times were few and far between.

As suddenly as it started, the rain stopped and the moon appeared from behind a cloud. Across the loch the lights of a town reflected in the water, and a car's headlamps spun like a searching beam across the sky as it struggled up the side of a hill. In the quiet, Dan could even make out the faint growl-like noise of the engine as the driver changed gears.

The bushes rustled as something made its way through the undergrowth. He stood still, alert and waiting, to be rewarded by the snuffle of a hedgehog. At least they didn't have any wallabies on Inchcondorran where the Department was based. Not like Inconnachan, a neighboring island where several of the marsupials had been brought seventy-odd years earlier. Having to check trip wires and cameras for wallaby interruptions would be a nightmare.

The hedgehog made its shuffling way past him and under another bush. With one last careful scan of the area, Dan continued on his path back to the house. Before he reached the building they all called HQ—on a good day, and all things unmentionable on a bad—Darke met him.

Darke. By name, nature and employment. The boss man of the island, but not— Dan knew, *the* boss man. Darke deferred to Crabtree—in some things, not all—and somewhere there was a higher authority, whom no one talked about. Dan didn't have a clue who he was and although he assumed Darke did, Darke wasn't telling.

It made it a mystery, and one that, on occasion, made Dan feel uncomfortable. After all if you were a puppet it was good to know who was pulling the strings.

"We're on red alert, and no I do not mean stop and do not go there." Darke smiled grimly. "Our ladies are not the sort to cry red, as I'm sure you know."

That was the first time Dan had heard any of the dispatchers mention their preferences in the bedroom. Or should that be playroom? He wondered if he'd ever have a chance to look inside, let alone use it. His room was in the main house, not anywhere the couples used. At first he'd felt left out. Now *he* accepted *he* had to be accepted in every area of living on the island before certain things were divulged to him.

"I guessed as much."

"Did you?" Darke stared at him intensely. "How perceptive of you. And?"

Dan shrugged. "Lucky bastards."

Darke laughed. "Sometimes. Would it help if I said your time will come?"

"Yeah, but I rather think it came and went when I got called up here," Dan said morosely, and sighed. "Ah well, into every life rain falls. Mine just decided to be a hurricane." He counted to three and made sure he spoke in a more upbeat way. "Anyhow, not your problem boss. I've pulled up my big boy boxers and got on with it."

"Just as well really." Darke clapped him on the shoulder. "Something is going down, we need you in the ops room. No cleaning up at the moment, but if you do get a chance for some shuteye, once you've been briefed,

I'd suggest you take it. Things might be about to get messy."

He didn't elaborate; however Dan hadn't expected him to. Even if it was never mentioned, and however much it annoyed him, he was on probation until he proved himself. Even though he knew he had been good at his job elsewhere, the dispatchers hadn't seen the evidence for themselves. Until then, therefore, as a dispatcher he was still an unknown entity.

Dan followed Darke into the building, and to their control room, ops room, ready room, or hell on earth, whoever chose to describe it. Several pairs of eyes stared at him. God he hated that experience. When all those bloody eyes seemed to have a life of their own, as if all the bodies they were in weren't paying him any attention. Just those fucking orbs of many colors.

"Something's going on," Michael, one of the other Dispatchers said flatly. "We all need to take a section and find out what the fuck it is. Someone seems to have broken through the security ring from the loch."

Darke stared at one of the computer screens on the wall and nodded. "Fuck it. Then this is what we'll do."

Within a few minutes only Dan and Michael were left in the control room. Michael handed Dan a coffee and punched him on the shoulder. "You look like shit. Been living it up eh?"

"Ha, as if." Dan took a large slurp and coughed. "Fucking hell! What is this? Iron filings. It's strong enough to pull out my fillings."

"Should have looked after your teggies as a kid. Then no fillings."

"Not likely really is it? What with humbugs, black bullets and pear drops."

"Black what? Sounds dangerous."

Dan grinned. "Ah I forgot it's not be known outside the northeast. One of my grans was a geordie. From Newcastle and it's a boiled sweet from there. I was addicted to them and a very chewy chew called fruit salads. Hence fillings. You got any?"

"Hell yeah, but I still like strong coffee."

"I guess I need it." Dan took another, more cautious sip. "Even if it does take the roof off my mouth. Working nights, takes it out of you, and yeah in a way, days as well."

"Trying to prove yourself?" Michael asked with sympathy. "Been there, done that and got the t-shirt. It takes time."

"I guess so." Dan shrugged. "Nah, I know so."

"Well don't stress *or* stress out. Take it from one who was a newbie not so long ago, no need. If you weren't worthy you wouldn't be here," Michael advised him. "You were recruited for whatever your special skills are. Don't knock it. You might think you get all the shitty jobs, but we all do at times. Until we're needed somewhere. You get me?"

Dan nodded, grateful for the reassurance he hadn't realized he needed. "Yeah, cheers. It's always hard hoping you'll fit in. And then to see you lot all so loved up, well…" He took a deep breath. He had to ask. "Lots of lovely necklaces your ladies wear. Very unusual."

Michael shot him a suspicious look. "Well what can I say… they all like jewelry." He essayed a devilish grin. "Unusual jewelry."

"And doing as you ask…when the time is right?"

Michael swiveled round from the computer screen he had been studying. "Spit it out."

"Are you all Doms?"

Michael narrowed his eyes. "Why does it matter?

Dan smiled. By not answering, Michael *had* responded in the affirmative. "It doesn't," Dan said equally. "Apart from inasmuch as, if I ever get me a sub again, I'll know you're all fine with it."

Michael stared at him for several seconds and then laughed. "Well, you'll fit in fine, mate. What the…?" He stared at his screen. "Shit, look at this. Bold as bloody brass, look." Someone walked across the lawn to the house and made no attempt to hide. "Fucking strange goings on."

"Yeah, want to me to head to the door?"

Michael nodded. "Don't open it until I give you the signal. I'll get it from Darke. Everyone knows what to do, where, how and when, and will report in when needed." It sounded complicated, but it wasn't. It just gave everyone space to work.

Dan put his earpiece in, and twiddled it until there was no distortion. As long as everyone didn't try to talk at once he'd be fine. The place was busier than Sauchiehall Street on an old firm football match day. "Sorted."

As he walked along the hallway, it sounded like the hounds of hell were shaking the main door of the house. He stood to one side of the bolt and waited.

"*Now.*" The voice was tinny in his ear.

"Copy." He swung the door open on silent hinges.

The intruder fell onto her—*what the fuck, it's a female*—knees.

"That's a nice way to be greeted. I love me a girl on her knees." Dan nudged her with his toes. "I think you better come in and greet everyone else in a more conventional way. Well?"

She looked up and glowered. Under the glare of the indoor light Dan got his first proper glimpse of her.

Shit. His heart missed a beat. *What the hell was* she *doing here?*

Dan did his best, a piss poor best, he decided, to laugh at her. "Conventional to most people. Here we prefer the sub on knees greeting."

"You? What the fuck are you doing here?" The girl poked him in the chest. "What the hell is all this eh? Where is he?"

Dan's eyes narrowed. "Enough, sweetness. Watch what you are saying or are you fond of a mouth washed out with soap?"

"Hell on wheels, have I had some weird and wonderful potion for my dinner? Making me hallucinate and see nasties?" She scrambled to her feet, ignored Dan's comments and fisted her hands into tight balls. "What have you done with my brother?"

She glanced around the hallway and appeared ready to do a serious injury to anyone who got in her way. "Where is he? Answer me, you bastard. The cops know I'm here."

"Bullshit about the cops. Why would they?"

"Cops are the good guys. I left a note with a friend. I don't trust it when people aren't open."

As the girl narrowed her eyes and balled her hands into fists, Dan thought maybe it was time to say something.

"Your brother, sweetness," Dan said, "is not here, and the boss man is waiting to talk to you about him. He's a bit like me, the boss man is. Not a patient person. I might know you and your brother. He doesn't."

"What?" The girl wiped her hands on her jeans. "Why?"

"I thought you'd know and tell me," Dan said. It was like being in a bloody nightmare with no idea why or how to get out of it. "Be honest."

"Why? You weren't," the girl said in a bitter voice. "Mr. I'm in the air force. I see no reason for helping a load of whatevers. Liars and stuff. Go on, do what you have to do and screw me over once more."

Paddle her ass if I got the chance would be a better ending. It was a pity; Dan didn't see that happening in the near future.

"Marcus Verene," he said. "Shall I spill the beans to the bossman and say you're Rhonda?"

"Fuck it, Dan, what the hell is going on here?" She spat out the words and then looked bewildered. "Where is he? The last I heard was he was doing marine biology for the government or something around here. No one's heard of him but I heard some guy in the village ask the post lady if he was about. She blew him off but I'd seen the bloke before, talking to Marcus years ago so I asked who he was. The woman in the post office was most chatty to me. Said she didn't know him, but lots of people worked for the government and lived on here. So." She shrugged. "Here I am and where's Marcus? He's all I've got now." Her eyes were bleak.

Dan put his hands in the air. What the hell was she going on about? He'd tried to explain, but how could you say, 'hey love, I work for a department that kills traitors and I'm off to hone my assassination skills. No idea where I'm going or for how long? Which beggared the question, 'who dumped who'? "Hey, bugger all to do with me, sweetness. You left. You flipped me the bird. I didn't throw my dummy out of the pram."

"You're the one whose fucking phone won't take a proper message or anything."

"Bullshit." But was it? Dan remembered his old phone had gone on the blink and his new one was very temperamental in this part of the country.

Rhonda burst into tears. "Argh, no. Shit, I hate

being a watering pot, but I need to see him."

"Don't we all." Crabtree appeared like a genie out of a bottle. "Why do you, specifically?"

"He's my bloody brother, that's why. Who are you?"

"Why do you want to see him?" Crabtree asked again.

"Not that's it got anything to do with you, Mr. No Name Mystery man, but I'm pregnant. Almost nine weeks. He'll know what I should do."

Dan saw black spots in front of him, and his skin became clammy. She was what? He did some rapid maths. "You bloody what?" His voice raised several notches before he took a deep breath and shook his head. "Not likely, sweetness."

Her expression was bleak. "If you say so. Anyway, I don't care what you say. Where's Marcus? He'll help me." Her eyes filled with tears. "Oh shit, I didn't mean to say that. I don't need him because I'm up the duff. I need him for something else. I'm confused."

"Now, I wonder why?" Dan said flatly. She was lying, he knew it. It was all to do with her pregnancy. "You, confused? That's a new phenomenon." God, she wasn't going to ask for help in arranging a termination, was she? It would be over his dead body, if she did. He turned on his heel and walked back towards the ops room. It was that or blot his copybook for ever.

Michael appeared from the ops room. "Shit eh? But all will be sorted out. I'll take the lady to my lady. She'll look after her for you."

"For me?" Dan asked. "It seems it's bugger all to do with me."

"For whoever then. All will be easily sorted."

"Yeah allegedly," Dan said. "If you believe that, I'll sell you whatever footie team you fancy for a knock down price."

"Footie's not my thing. No, weird beliefs. I feel it in my water."

"Ha, and what does your lady say to that?" Dan asked, grateful Michael tried to lighten the atmosphere.

"When I have feelings in my water?' Michael guffawed. "My lady? She tells me to drink more cranberry juice."

That sounded like Lindsey, Michael's lady. Dan shook his head as Michael clapped him on the shoulder. "Does she say add vodka?"

"No, but I live in hope. By the way, Dan. You're needed in the small sitting room."

Dan nodded. He had to clear his head somehow, and the few minutes it would take to get there would, he hoped, help him a little. His sort of ordered life had taken a massive 'u' turn, and he had no idea what the hell was going on. As he hated mess and uncertainty, it was not a comfortable experience. "'kay, on my way."

Darke asked the same question that was annoying Dan. "Do you have any clues as to where bloody Marcus Verene is?"

Dan thought for a moment. He didn't know Verene that well, and what he had gleaned about the man came from Rhonda, who had done her best—not always with a lot of success—to be impartial. "I reckon if he was around here, he's long gone. He's a shit. Rhonda has never really asked for his help. He ignores her until *he* wants something and now that she's the one in need, the fucker has ignored her. Evidently he was an all round good bloke until his wife was murdered. Now he's embittered."

"Some bastards are ready to screw anyone as long as it's for their own best interest," Darke said. "We'll find him somehow, and Dan, you're needed elsewhere. Best go. There's nothing else we can do except be on our guard. Keep your walkie talkie handy."

Dan nodded. "I'm rostered on duty anyway, so I won't be long."

"Nope, you've been swapped. As of now. You'll be more use elsewhere." Darke didn't spell out where. There was no need.

Chapter Three

Rhonda looked at the door for at least the tenth time and wondered what on earth she'd done. After half an hour in the small sitting room, her nerves had got the better of her and her upchuck system and she'd retired to the room she'd been given—to throw up in the loo, clean her teeth, shower and then get into bed. She was dog tired, antsy, and not able to relax.

Around her the silence of the house, the deep velvet comfort of the very early morning, surrounded her like it was her own personal security blanket. Warm welcoming, loving, silence.

It did what nothing else had…made her relax. Sadly not sleep, but take away the tension headache and aching limbs. What would be, would be. Rhonda sat up in bed; she tugged the borrowed nightie well down over her legs and stared at the man who silently entered the room. If she hadn't been subconsciously waiting for him, she wouldn't have noted his presence.

"You always did move like a cat," she said as she hugged her knees. "To what do I owe this displeasure?"

Dan smiled like the cat she'd just likened him to and sat on the end of the bed. "What do you think?"

Rhonda shrugged, as insouciantly as she could. "Honestly? I've no idea. I came to look for Marcus. You were the last person I expected to see. This island's a bit small for an air force base isn't it?" She sighed. "An air force base. Sheesh, gullible or what. Wanna sell me a bridge? What is it with me, that no bloody one ever tells me the truth? Do I have 'use as a mug' tattooed on my forehead or something?"

"Don't talk daft. I couldn't tell you."

Rhonda rolled her eyes. "And that's a cop out if I ever heard one. Now let's screw her senseless, play

Master and…"

He grabbed her arm. Not tightly and not to give pain, but to show his displeasure, she decided.

"No playing, sweetness. I was, and am your Master and don't ever think otherwise. I might not be able to paddle your ass or show you my displeasure in the way I'd prefer, but I can remember for later."

"Only if I agree," she said as she tried to ignore the way her pulse sped up and her body tightened in anticipation. "And I don't."

"Liar, but I'll let it go for now."

Rhonda sighed and hated how much hurt she could put into that one sound. It was pathetic. "I don't think, so, Dan. I know you left. That means it's over in my book."

"Not in mine. I had no option."

To her everlasting relief he didn't add, 'and you said no more contact, not me'. Even though it was true, and she had acted like a spoiled brat, she didn't need reminding of it. "You hurt me." Rhonda cursed the plaintive note in her voice. It made her sound a whiny cow. "It was all hunky dory one minute, and thanks for good sex, I'm off now the next."

"It was more than sex," Dan said. "The rest? I know, pet, and I'm sorry. I intend to spend the rest of my life atoning for it, and showing you how you are my life."

"You said that before." How she wanted to accept his words, but she needed more. Rhonda didn't know what, exactly, just more.

"I'm saying it again. I'll keep on saying it until you believe me."

"I believed everything you said last time. Shit, I must be the only person in the world who fell for such a stupid excuse," she said bitterly. "'Sorry, it's secret', she parroted. "It's a wonder you didn't add that old chestnut, 'if I did I'd have to kill you afterwards'."

He laughed. "There's more than one way to die, sweetness."

"Yeah, well at the moment I don't want you to do either to me. I feel such a bloody fool." Rhonda got up out of bed and began to pace. It gave her some satisfaction to know how much he hated her doing that. He'd told her often enough in the past when...

Do not go there. That thought was enough to get her riled again.

"Any more lies you want to tell me?" she demanded as she swung around to stand in front of him. If she'd hoped he'd feel at a disadvantage sitting down whilst she stood, she now realized she was wrong. In her borrowed nightie, she was the one disadvantaged. Every time she moved, Tweety Pie, the silly cartoon bird printed on the material, seemed to stroke her pussy.

I wish it was him stroking me.

Dan sat left ankle over his right knee, with his well worn, white at the seam denims lovingly outlining every contour, and smiled in that 'melt her ire, make her want to kneel at his feet and do whatever he demanded' way. She couldn't leave it alone though. Surely it was better to say everything that had been building up inside her since she last saw him?

"You know, 'oh you're the sub for me, I need you only you', crap."

That did make him stand up. In one fluid motion he towered over her. Six feet four to her five feet three. She'd roused the tiger. A swift bolt of arousal, fear and excitement coursed through her. Whatever happened next would perhaps cement her future. Hers and their child's.

"You're pregnant with my child. I didn't know, now I do and you expect me not to be pissed, surprised, taken aback, or whatever? Just say 'okay then, what next' and not wonder about things? Not ask for explanations, but sit back and wait for you to decide if and how I get involved? Oh, pet you are so, so wrong about it all. Think again."

Dan folded his arms across his chest and stared at her. His face became a blank canvas and nothing showed of how he felt, or what else he intended to say. He drew the silence out, until Rhonda was ready to say something...anything, just to nudge him into a reply. She opened her mouth and he shook his head.

"My turn still. I might have been economical with the truth at other times, but never with regard to that. You are the only sub I want. The only woman if it comes to that. It half crucified me when I left, but think back. You told me to go and not to bother you again. It was good while it lasted you said, but enough was enough. You chose that. I would have gotten back to you as soon as I could."

His patient, 'believe me or not, I can't do or say anymore to convince you' tones deflated her anger. Rhonda sighed. "I know, I'm sorry. Put it down to pregnancy hormones."

"For now. But we will talk about our future, make no bones about that."

She hoped he meant future together. "Yes, I want to." Did his expression soften? She couldn't tell. "But, Dan, apart from you, me, and bump to make three, I am worried about my brother. He's missing, and well, I honestly thought I'd find him around here."

"Why?"

Did he stare at her a bit too intently? A horrible slither of fear slid up her spine and gave her an unpleasant tingle across her scalp. "Why what?"

"Come on Rhonda, stop playing games; this is

important. Why did you think you'd find him here?"

The intent look as he focused on her would have had her on her knees if she wasn't so bloody worried. "Well not necessarily here at first. Until I heard people talking about the place. But he'd sent me a card of the loch, and this island was slap bang in the middle of the picture, so it seemed as good a place as any to start. He's..." She hesitated but maybe now wasn't the time or place for sibling loyalty. "You know he's been bitter since his wife died and was convinced it was down to a guy called Crabtree for not responding to a known threat early enough. He also mentioned a few other names, and when I heard someone in the village mention Darke, I remembered that was one of the names Marcus had sworn about when he was half drunk, and thought it was worth sussing this out. Then I saw some of you and so here I am."

"One of us mentioned Darke?" Dan's expression was one of fury. "Someone's in for it, if they did."

Rhonda hurried to disabuse him of that idea. "What? Oh no, someone in the post office did to the lady who sold the stamps. No one I've noticed here."

"Do you know who?"

She shook her head. "Never seen him before. A weasly-faced bloke with ginger hair. About five six, a bit flabby and not Scottish. London or Essex I reckon, definitely no further north." Her linguistics degree, with its dialectology lectures, came in handy sometimes. "Asked if Mr. Darke had been in lately. The woman just looked at him, and said she had no idea. I guessed she was being discreet."

"You, my pet, are brilliant." Dan kissed her long and hard.

Rhonda enjoyed the moment, his scent and his presence. She guessed it would be all she had for a while.

She was right. Even before she'd had time to register how right it seemed, Dan drew back. Both breathed heavily.

"A…damn. Save that thought. Look, do you feel up to coming down and telling the others all about this?"

"As long as I can get dressed." She tugged at the too-tight nightie. God knows what it revealed, but she'd hazard a guess: more than it covered.

Dan grinned. "Pity, that Tweety Pie on the front is rather cute. Except he's got his mouth where I want mine." He winked. "Okay, sorry." He held his hands in front of him as she made a fist. "Yep, you get dressed and I'll ring Darke to let him get everyone from wherever they might be. Upset a few couples no doubt but tough. Needs must."

"Upset how?"

He held his hand in the air as the phone was answered. Rhonda watched, as he blinked, appeared somewhat startled and then whistled. "Eh? Fuck no? When? Ah right. Soon as shit, okay five minutes or so." Then he switched his mobile off and tapped it on his teeth.

"You'll break something."

"Hmm? Yes, sorry. Thinking here. Darke says after I was told to come and make my peace with you— his words not mine. Mine are more ask if you can ever see your way to being mine again, and I'll wait as long as I have to—he gave some startling and unpleasant news to the rest, and said to take an hour or so to come to terms with it. So, he'll get back who ever he can. I'd say it's a given conclusion that some people thought to get a wee bit of playing in, and whereas no one would be interrupted if their sub was in sub space, I bet there will be a few sore asses that need rubbing. This was one of the times it would be nothing too deep, nothing too strong, and definitely nothing that takes very long."

Rhonda knew her lips twitched, even though it really wasn't a time for hilarity. After all, what sort of unpleasant news did he impart? And why hadn't Dan shared it with her? Did he even know? She forced herself not to ask, but concentrated on what else had been said. "Darke a poet?"

He grimaced. "Nope. Darke's idea of being funny. Okay, my pet. Dress as fast as you can, and I'll wait for you. Whatever is going on, Darke's not in the best of fettle."

You could say that again, Rhonda thought a short while later. They, along with most of the members of The Dispatchers and partners, except for two of the ladies, who were, it was explained, on babysitting duties, crowded into a too small conference room.

"If we were staying here this would need to be enlarged," Astrid, Darke's lady said, and then appeared visibly startled. "What? What have I said?"

"Nothing yet, babe, so keep it that way for now, eh? Maybe explain a bit about you and your father? Just so Rhonda knows what's going on."

"I'm here as my dad is, somehow, we think, your brother's target," Astrid said as she sat down next to Darke. "Dad was here, had to go and well…Oh okay."

Darke coughed theatrically and Astrid looked at him in a quizzical way. "Hey, we're not all mind readers, you know. Someone had to explain why some people are missing."

"As you say, and this should be easier, now. After all, the main protagonists…with the exception of Crabtree, who is, shall we say, busy sorting traps out, and hopefully will help us to get to the end of all this, are safe."

It sounded ominous, and Rhonda was as

confused as hell. Except for one thing. "If you're talking about my brother, then he's no killer," Rhonda said, as she held back her anger. How dare he suggest such a thing? "A grief stricken man, yes, and I'm sure one with a grudge, but I can't see him killing anyone in cold blood."

"Pet." Dan touched her arm. "If he hasn't done it himself, he's instigated it. Which is just as bad."

"You have proof of this?" She spun around and glared at Darke who stood, arms folded, and leaned against the wall. "Show me, irrefutable proof?"

"Your brother sent people to kill Astrid, because they couldn't reach Crabtree, or me," Darke said flatly. " One of those is still around, and as far as our intelligence goes, still determined to kill her, Crabtree or me."

Now, it all began to make horrific sense. "A scruffy, weasely-faced bloke with ginger hair? Maybe five foot six tall and a bit flabby."

Darke exchanged looks with Astrid. "Local?" he asked. "Where?"

Rhonda shook her head as she puzzled over what that complicated exchange of looks could mean. "Definitely not a Scottish accent. London or Essex I thought, and like I said to Dan, I'm certain he's not from further north. Not even a hint of elsewhere, and most people pick up the odd word or two."

Darke appeared skeptical.

"My degree is in linguistics and I studied accents. I know I'm right. If we ever have time I'll listen to you all and bet I can pinpoint where you lived longest to within a tiny area."

"I'll hold you to that," Astrid said. "It could be interesting. But as my Sir is glaring, go on about the man."

"I saw him in that village on the shores of the

loch, before I found out how to get here."

"Which village, Luss?"

Rhonda shook her head. "Other side. Bally something."

"Balmaha," Dan said. "Where that postcard that shows here is most often sold."

Astrid went white and shook Darke's arm. "Mr X," she said in a faint voice. "The one who stayed in the background. The one we keep hearing about, who you say has gone rogue. Him. And oh god, *Dad.* You let Dad go to the mainland." She began to pace. "We need to warn him."

"Gone rogue?" Rhonda whispered to Dan. She moved even closer to him, so her thigh was pressed to his. Not even a gnat could have squeezed between them. "What does she mean? How?"

Darke must have overheard. "I've just got the information that your brother called off his minions, but this one refused to give in. Look, a lot has happened and now as the Dispatchers in theory no longer exist, it's hard to get information quickly."

Rhonda decided her head hurt. One minute she was being told about this elite group, and what they did, the next that they didn't exist. "Can someone explain?" she asked. "Is my brother in trouble or not?"

"Yes he is," Darke said flatly.

Well that told her.

"And what about Weasel Willie? If he's gone out on his own, how could that be put down to Marcus?" The nasty sensation of pregnancy's any-time-of-the-day sickness about to hit made her clammy. Astrid pressed a bottle of water into her hand and pushed a packet of ginger biscuits closer.

"Nibble and sip."

Rhonda was more than grateful to do as she was

told. "Better, sorry," she said when she decided she could talk and not spew. "I keep getting told it will pass, but then I was told it was morning sickness as well."

"Nah, wherever and whenever it wants to be sickness and it might or might not pass. I've got some wristbands you can have. Only thing that helped me."

Darke smiled. Not the usual saturnine expression that Rhonda had seen, but a softer, more loving countenance, that she guessed he reserved for Astrid and his children. "As soon as we get this sorted, babe, okay, we'll get thinking about when you next need them. Sorry, Rhonda, I have to ask who you mean."

Beside Rhonda, Dan moved suddenly. "I suspect my pet means the guy gone rogue."

Rhonda saw more than one speculative expression turn to understanding at what, she was inclined to think, was a deliberate turn of phrase from Dan. It seemed more than she and her Sir were, or had been involved in, some of the same things she and Dan enjoyed. *Or we did enjoy.* Who knew if she'd get the chance to enjoy them again? How complicated did that sound? Kinksters all?

"Willie will do for a code name," Darke said. "I believe his actual name is Fred Hatchett—very apt in the circumstances—and indeed he was born and bred in Essex. Good listening, Rhonda."

She inclined her head. "So what now?"

"Now, we plot how to find him, find your brother, find what the hell is going on, and why The Dispatchers were disbanded. Somehow, I think they are all linked."

"I thought you said tomorrow to be disbanded?" Dan asked. "So how come we get nothing now?"

"Because it all stinks," Darke said. "Because someone is fucking with us. And when I find out who..."

He didn't need to finish his sentence.

Chapter Four

Dan stretched out, crossed his ankles and watched as Darke opened the door and closed it again. "Much as I love them, I don't trust our ladies not to leave someone listening at the keyhole. I'll check outside in a sec. Inventive is their middle names. And this is something we need to hash out before they get involved." He turned his chair around and straddled it before he leaned on the back of it. "Maddock is on his way in. Mason is still following up some lead or another." They were both dispatchers and a couple. "That ditsy persona of Mason's comes in handy at times. Maddock says we will need a lure."

Dan had that awful hard lump of dread in his stomach. The one he got before something unpleasant, not to say scary, went down. He could almost see the cogs in Darke's mind whirring around.

Not a great feeling. Dan took a quick glance around the room. Every male who lived on the island, apart from Maddock, was there. He didn't count anyone temporarily housed in the cells. Even Crabtree, who was as he put it, a temporary resident, sat on one of the chairs around the table.

Dan stood up and helped himself to a mug of coffee, and some sort of sticky, and no doubt unhealthy bun, as Maddock slipped in via the window.

"One subbie needs a lesson in doing what she's told," he said, as he straddled the window ledge, stepped down into the room, and reached back outside. "Not mine for a change."

"Whose?" Every man in the room spoke at once.

Maddock shrugged. "Not a clue. Whoever it was is fucking good though, because okay I wasn't doing the total stealth bit but nor was I clumping along. I only caught a glimpse of someone as I reached the edge of the first group of trees."

"Are you sure it was one of our ladies though?" Darke persisted. "Could it have been anyone else?"

"Ah." It was obvious Maddock hadn't thought of that. "Shit. It could have been I suppose, but as I hadn't heard about any breach of security on here, and the figure was slight, I thought it was one of the girls. *Has* there been a breach?"

Michael shook his head. "The only in or out was your bo...ah... anyone know what sort of swimmer or diver Willie the Weasel is?"

"Now, as none of us actually know the bloke well, how would we?" Dan asked in a reasonable voice. "But I'd sure like to find out."

"Willie the... Oh you mean Fred Hatchettt," Darke said. "He can't swim, or he couldn't when he did his basic training. One reason why he never got any further than he did."

"And one more reason to have a grudge against you and yours?" Maddock said. "Or whoever he works for has?"

Darke frowned. "I guess so."

Dan cleared his throat. "Could it be Marcus Verene?" He almost wished he hadn't voiced his thoughts as everyone turned to stare at him.

"Elucidate," Maddock said without any embellishment. "What do you know that we might not?"

"I don't *know* anything, but I just wondered. If he is around, surely he'd have found out that his sister is here? And if he has also got hold of the info that Rho and I were once an item, and somehow we've hooked up again...well..." He grimaced. "If he's kept an eye on her, would that mean he'd try to get to her?"

"There's worse," Michael said as he looked up from his phone. "Just got an encrypted message from, well from someone, and it appears Hatchett is following Verene. He blames Verene for all his later problems."

It was getting ever more complicated. "Then do we know who wants who disposed of then?" Dan asked as he hugged Rhonda. It couldn't be easy for her to hear this. "Do I need to lock my lady somewhere safe?"

Darke smirked. "If she's anything like the rest of our ladies, in your dreams or in your playroom maybe. Got your handcuffs handy?"

Dan snorted. "Sadly no. I thought any chance of using them was long gone." He didn't say that all his tools were locked away under his bed. That was for him to know and no one else. "I just have a dart board and a set of darts."

"Fair enough. We'll have to put it up in the games room next to the pool table."

Michael guffawed. Darke scowled. "Not that room and you know it." Darke threw something at Dan, which he caught automatically. It was a small key. "To the playroom. Last door at the end of the top corridor. Each and every one of us have been through that scenario, believe you me. Help yourself to anything you need. If you want the room, there's an app to book it. Ask Milo."

Rhonda snorted. "Maybe ask me as well?"

Dan glanced at her. "Why? You going to say no, pet?"

She grinned. "Hell, no. Ooops I just did."

"You do realize that I'm the only one who doesn't need your room, don't you?" Crabtree said plaintively. "Or anything in it. And even though I know my daughter is happy, I'd prefer not to have any details."

"Not gonna give you any," Darke said promptly.

"And no time anyway. Milo, what do we need to know?"

There was a commotion in the corridor outside. Dan noted the various expressions that flickered across his fellow dispatchers' faces. Darke raised his eyebrows so high they almost disappeared under his receding hairline and sighed. It was more resigned than sad. "Who's gonna do the honors?"

Maddock grinned. "I'll go and... ah no need." The door opened and three of the ladies entered.

"Is it time for bed yet?" Mason asked. "'Cos it's getting on a bit, and I need some shut-eye for a while. Can we sort rostas out, and ohh we need to relieve the others from babysitting duties. Other boobies are needed."

Astrid patted her chest and laughed. "I'm on my way."

Darke shoved his chair back. "Two hourly stints in twos. Maddock, can you sort it? Dan, you take your lady to rest, see her settled and come back here for a while."

Rhonda stood up as there was a general shift of people. Dan took hold of her hand. "Come on, pet, like the man says time for you to try to get some rest. We have no idea what's going to happen, and need to be as alert as possible when the time comes." He waited until they were climbing the stairs to her room, his as well, if she did but know it. "Are you my pet again?"

Rhonda glanced at him. "Maybe, Sir." She wiggled her bum. "Maybe not."

Dan laughed and patted the said bum. "Minx. All brattiness will be duly remembered."

"Ooh good. Now what else can I do to get on to the spanking list?"

"Be mine?" Dan stopped as they reached the landing, and pulled her close. "When we have time to talk, my pet, we will do just that. Our future, the future of our child," he patted her belly and caressed it in a gentle circular motion, "that's too important to mess up. Now, will you be okay by yourself for a while?"

Rhonda nodded. "I'd rather snuggle with you, but needs must. Yes, Sir, we'll talk later."

****

It was much later when they talked.

"I came for you, kitten—just you. To show you what you're missing, to show you what we both need, and..." Dan's voice lowered into that sexy subtle Dom-like cadence that made her go weak at the knees, "to show you how much I care." They were both naked. His cock rubbed against her ass, and his fingers tweaked her oh so sensitive nipples. "To show my sweet pet what we both need."

When he spoke like that it was all she could do not to slide onto the floor and beg his forgiveness. Only the thought of the precious bundle she carried inside stopped her.

Was it real? She hoped so.

"Explain, will you?" she asked breathlessly. "Why now?"

"In case I don't get a chance later. In case something happens. In case you didn't know how much I love you, and I never got the chance to tell you."

Hell, she didn't like the sound of that. "I love you too, Sir. In every way. But what aren't you telling me?"

"There's a killer on the loose and he's not getting you."

That was all she needed. Rhonda opened her mouth...

It was covered by his... Soft, persuasive, and...*shit hell and buggery.* Why was he shaking her, not spanking her? She opened her eyes and pouted.

"I was enjoying all that," Rhonda complained. "It was getting oh so interesting, and I want more. I'm pregnant, not ill. I've read up on it. What's safe and what's not."

Dan pinched her clit. "You'll get more, I promise. As soon as you're at the...what is it? Second trimester? We have time and no enemies to drag us out of our own special scene, and can enjoy everything. Now though, we need to get up and go over the plan. I've just had the alert from Darke. Your brother is definitely on the island and so is Hatchett. I need to go down to the ops rom. Are you sure you'll be okay with the others while I go and do my bit for queen and country?"

"Well, duh. I'm a big girl." She patted her tummy. "And gonna get bigger. Me and bump will stay here, or be with the others. Astrid did say we'd stick together."

"I'd imagine she's got everything under control." Dan dressed rapidly as he spoke and shoved his feet into heavy boots.

When did he get naked? I thought it was a dream?

Obviously not.

"Okay, sweet, I better go." Dan kissed Rhonda on the nose. "Lock the door and..."

"Don't open it until you know who's outside," she said as she gave Dan a swift hug. "I promise. Having found us again I don't intend to lose us." She wrinkled her nose. "Does that make sense? Well, you know what I mean."

"I do and ditto." Dan left the room. "Lock the door," he said as he shut it behind him.

Rhonda giggled as she did as he asked, and then leaned back on the door. This sense of being cherished was oh so good; she had no intention of doing anything to upset it.

The silence had a menacing quality to it, and it didn't help her skittering nerves. Her phone tinged and she jumped. It was only a message from Dan. 'Stay put. Astrid in lockdown as well. Will keep in touch.' Then within seconds a message from Astrid herself. 'This sucks and sadly not a dick.'

That made Rhonda laugh and reply, 'no dicks in sight.'

Which was all very well, but she'd come up without the Kindle Emma had loaned her, and her phone was new with no Kindle app yet installed. She held it at all angles. No internet.

Sod it. What now? Calisthenics? Gentle yoga for mums to be? Rhonda mooched into the ensuite bathroom and stared at the shelf above the loo. Then she blinked and snorted. The shelf was empty, apart from two tiny boxes. Both had curly writing on them. One said 'pussypeach', and the other 'redasmyass'. There was a Post-it note between them. 'Your choice, pet.'

She chose 'redasmyass'. After all it was probably the nearest to a red ass she'd get for a few months.

The damned stuff must have been bought in a ten year past its sell by date sale. It took her ages to unscrew the lid and then the brush wouldn't move. Rhonda swore under her breath and wandered round the room. She could do with a needle or a pin or something to try and loosen the brush. A swift search of the three drawers in the bathroom produced a cuff link, a new toothbrush and weirdly a tiny bottle of sun cream. Factor 30, which in this part of Scotland would be needed about three days a year. Probably why it was only a small bottle.

The bedroom wardrobe was no better. Then she noticed the dartboard propped up against the wall. Could she wrench a bit of the wire mesh off? She didn't have to. Sellotaped to the back of it was a shining, new-looking set of darts and right or wrong, they even had their flights attached. She couldn't have asked for more.

Rhonda un-taped them and slipped them into her pocket before she went back to the bed and began to wrestle with the stuck bottle top. Whether it had slackened due to her previous attempts or what, she didn't know, but of course the top opened with ease.

She began to apply the varnish with care. How long before she wouldn't be able to see her toes to paint them anymore? Maybe, if she and Dan did stay together she could persuade him to do it instead? The thought of persuading Dan to do anything he didn't want to made her grin. Not a Scooby's chance. Then a scene from an old movie, where the baseball playing hero painted the heroine's toenails, made her smile. That guy was a macho man if ever there was one. Maybe she could appeal to Dan's inner sensitivity? *Ha, in my dreams. Maybe appeal to his Master side instead. That should work.*

Rhonda hummed to herself and concentrated as she reached her littlest toe. She never found it easy to keep to the nail, not the skin. Why she was humming an oldie called 'Eve of Destruction' she had no idea, and hoped it wasn't an omen.

Stop it now. She changed the humming to whistling, 'Let Me Entertain You.' How she wished.

The knock at the door made her jump and leave a trail of 'redasmyass' polish over her toe, foot and the coverlet.

Sod it to hell. Should she shout or stay quiet? About to yell and ask who was outside, a creeping crawling slither of nasties made her stop and shut her mouth. Surely if it was friend *not* foe they would say so.

Then she heard a familiar voice. "Rhon? Don't open the argh... Ar... sh..."

"If you don't open the door I'll kill him." This voice she didn't recognize. Who was it? "Your choice. Come out and give me leverage or...he gets it. I've done it before, I'll do it again."

"Rhon ignore... I'm dead anyway, don't do it."

Marcus. God help me.

She scanned the room intently. How could she let someone safe know what was going on, without giving away she was in there, to whoever were outside? At least she was barefooted, but what was the good of that if she couldn't go anywhere? Very carefully she walked across the carpet, into the bathroom, and opened the window. As she hoped it didn't squeak or scrape, but with a straight twenty-ish feet of pebbledash between it and the tarmac below, there wasn't a cat in hell's chance she could get out that way.

What now?

Rhonda stared around the tiny space for inspiration. Outside the door, the noises had stopped, which to her mind, was more ominous than the threats. Where was her mobile? She'd put it down to choose nail varnish... with a heartfelt sigh of relief she spied it on the top of the cistern.

Who to text? She'd deleted Dan's number in a fit of pique when he'd left her, something that seemed reasonable then, and she decided was an overreaction now, and he wasn't the one to text anyway. However. She screwed her eyes up in concentration, and peered carefully around the door into the bedroom. Shit, she swore the door was opening.

Hopefully she'd remembered Dan's number, but whatever it was worth a try. Rhonda typed one word... 'baddyhere', and sent it to the number she'd dredged from her memory. Heaven help her if it was wrong.

There was nowhere she could hide...or was there? Was that a narrow door in the wall beside the shower? With her luck it was probably the cupboard for the water tank or the plumbing. Even so, she pressed on one edge and wanted to high five when it swung open and she glanced inside, to see a tiny empty space. It was better than nothing. Very quietly she eased into the cupboard and thanked her lucky stars she was only a few months pregnant, not full term. A nine month-shaped tum wouldn't have got through the aperture.

She closed it, used her phone for a second to see that, for some strange reason, the cupboard locked from the inside, and pushed the bolt over.

And waited.

It wasn't a moment too soon. Even cocooned in her hidey-hole she heard her brother's voice.

"See? She's not here. So kill me already, unless you don't have the guts."

Then there was silence.

Rhonda moved her shoulders the three inches needed for her to lean back on the wall opposite the door. She thought the air would be stuffy, the darkness absolute. To her everlasting relief it was neither. Above her head, a tiny grating let a little of fresh air and pale moonlight in. It still didn't aid her in her predicament though. A possible killer outside, no idea if her text had managed to get to anyone, let alone Dan, and she was stuck in a cupboard. Very carefully, Rhonda wriggled to move something that stuck into her back.

It felt like a.... Rhonda inched around and used her fingers to discover what it was, and gave a silent 'yee ha.' Another bolt. This one was smaller and she had to fumble around as she did her best to open it without any noise.

Now she had to answer the knotty question of whether to open it or not.

What had she to lose?

Her life?

What had she to gain?

Her brother's life?

It was a no brainer.

"Come out Rhonda, he's a goner if you don't."

Rhonda took a deep breath and counted to ten.

She recognized the voice.

Chapter Five

Dan followed Mac, one of the senior operatives, along one of the tracks that led toward the shoreline. With the skill of an experienced operative, Mac showed him how to bypass the snares and traps left for any infiltrator and how to check if they had been activated. If nothing else it showed to Dan how he was now trusted.

"We should have done this during the day, and given you a chance to assimilate it easier, but things got out of hand faster than any of us anticipated," Mac said as he examined a camera. "This one's okay. You're well on track, mind you. Darke asked me to reassure you of that."

"Not much consolation if we're being disbanded though, is it?" Dan said, as he noted what switch to move on the tiny hidden camera to reset it. "Seems crackers to me."

Mac gave him a sharp glance. "I didn't think you were daft."

"Should I have added 'allegedly'?" Dan had wondered how calm everyone had seemed when he'd been given the news, well after the rest of them had. Not for any nefarious reason, but because he'd been with Rhonda. He hadn't thought it was because they'd had time to assimilate the information, but as the last in, he didn't think it had been his place to ask more questions. Not until he understood all the nuances of Darke's terse message.

"'Allegedly' is as good a way as any of putting it, I guess. Allegedly we are no more. In reality, here we are trying to find out who's fucking us over. Ah... a clue. Shit, I sound like that Belgian detective bloke, or Sherlock." He bent and picked up a tiny slither of wood, no bigger than a sewing needle.

"No shit, Sherlock, how the hell did you see that?"

Mac laughed. "Moon lit it up for a split second. But I reckon it's from the old landing stage. The one that if you go near the middle is designed to tip you in the water. Let's go there via a circular route."

Dan nodded, content to let the expert lead the way. He wondered what was going on back at the house. On cue, his phone reverberated against his thigh and he fished it out, before he shielded the screen to read the message.

'Baddyhere'

"Mac," he spoke in the level undertone they all adopted for secrecy. "Trouble. We've got to go back"

Mac spun around. "What?"

"Rhonda. She's texted. Baddyhere. We need to go back now. He began to move until Mac grabbed him by the waist of his camo trousers to stop him. Dan struggled, but Mac was three inches taller, broader and harder.

"Get off you fucker I need to go, that's my lady and my unborn child in danger."

"And every other lady and already born baby," Mac said, in a 'don't diss with me' tone. "Let me tell Darke and Maddock, they're closer. Then we make sure we cut off any escape routes. Hell, mate, I know you want to be there, so do I. But we're dispatchers so we suck it up and don't fuck it up."

As Dan heard the anguish Mac hadn't managed to hide he did his best to calm down. He wasn't the only one with loved ones in jeopardy. Dan took a deep breath and sought to inject some lightheartedness into his reply. "Bugger, I thought we were ex dispatchers."

"Never an ex in there I reckon. Hold on." Mac

spoke rapidly into a tiny microphone attached to his shirt, in a language Dan didn't understand. "Right. That's them in the know, and they'll put everything needed into action."

"In gobbledygook?"

"Esperanto. You'll need to learn it. As an ex dispatcher. We need to go to the landing stage and set the trip wires. Milo and Rio are doing the north end. Darke said to say he'll make sure your lady is safe and sound."

Mac didn't add the dreaded, 'if he can'. Dan took it as read. He forced down his panic. He was a dispatcher because it was expected he could handle danger. So now it was time to show he could.

"Copy," he said in the same monotone Mac used.

"That's it mate, come on, let's get this secured and see what next."

They resumed their circular route to the old landing stage. Three yards before thy reached the edge of the trees, Mac stopped dead.

"There's someone there."

Dan edged forward to peer over Mac's shoulder. "Who?"

"No idea but not one of us, that's for sure. What the hell is he doing?" The figure had put a long bulky package down on the wooden planks and was bent over as he fished for something under the top rail.

"Looking for a boat?"

"Under there?"

It did seem a bit weird but who knew? "Well why not, if it's a canoe."

"Good thinking... Now who the hell is that?" Another figure approached from the east, openly and without trying to hide.

He—or she—whistled and the person on the landing stage spun around. "What do you want?"

Dan and Mac watched in silence as the second person crunched over the shingle to the edge of the loch.

"Stay back." Now the voice held more than a hint of panic in it. "Don't come any closer or I'll kick him in." Person one nudged the package at his feet with one boot shod foot. "He's stuck in there. They say drowning isn't pleasant when you can't tell what's happening. Poor old Marcus won't have a clue, until he realizes that I won in the end."

"Marcus Verene?" Mac asked Dan in an undertone. "Why him now? Just because he's Rhonda's brother? But why her, then?"

Then who the hell was the other person? Dan got the 'oh fuck I'll kill her' itch up his spine. "No idea," he said softly. "But what's the betting that's Rhonda on the beach somehow?"

"No bets...shhh, let's see what's going on and what we need to do." Marcus indicated a nearby bush, several yards closer to the beach. They moved with stealth to secret themselves behind it.

"A pity I can't do away with you as well, you sod," the would-be killer said in a voice that sent shivers down Dan's spine. "You're as bad. Always sticking up for him. I was oh so surprised to realize you were here as well. Happily surprised. Two for one. How did you get out of that room, anyway? "

"Me to know, you to wonder, Gracie," Rhonda said. If you hadn't listened intently you would never have heard the tremor in her voice. "Yes I recognize you. I wonder why I didn't know that weasely-faced bloke was you. I should have remembered you were well up for amateur dramatics." She laughed, a bit shaky but still a laugh. "You were never that good, were you?"

Gracie howled. "I bloody was."

Rhonda shrugged. "If you say so. No one else

does though. Bet you hate that, don't you? But you know, I didn't realize you hated Marcus. What's he ever done to you?"

"Got my sister killed."

"Rubbish. She was in the wrong place at the wrong time. These things unfortunately happen."

"No, she shouldn't have been there. I told her: don't go to the uni that day. She laughed and said it was fine. I knew it wasn't because he," Gracie nudged the bundle again, "he didn't get his group of so called do-gooders sorted. They turned me down." Her voice rose to a high-pitched shriek. "Me, who knew about things."

Mac glanced at Dan. Dan shrugged. He had no bloody clue. Out of the corner of his eye he watched, as Rhonda took a tiny step closer to the landing stage, and then another.

Be careful, love.

Gracie pushed the bundle—Marcus Verene—Dan surmised—to the edge of the dock, and stood next to it. "They were supposed to take me in to be one of them, and I was going to solve the whereabouts of the bomb. Easy, as I saw it put there. Then it would all have gone the way it should. Not now."

"But, Gracie, that had nothing to do with Marcus, you know." Rhonda used the tone of voice a mother would use to soothe a fractious child. "Why are you blaming him?"

"He was her husband; he should have stopped her going. I told him. I bloody told him not to let her go. And now she's dead, so he needs to die as well. I wanted you to see, let you understand what it's like."

She sounded so rational it gave Dan goose bumps.

"So say good bye to Marcus." She started to kick Marcus over the edge.

"Nooooooo!" Rhonda began to run, at the same time as Dan and Mac. Something silver and gold flashed in the moonlight. Gracie screamed, held her hand to her cheek and stumbled backward off the dock. There was a noise like thunder as the weakened planks split in half and Gracie tumbled though them.

"I can't swim," Gracie yelled as Rhonda ran past her.

"Tough." Rhonda reached the edge of the loch at the same time as Mac and Dan. Dan held her as she struggled to get into the water.

"Let Mac do it. He'll go for Marcus, I promise. Will you stay here if I go for her? I'd rather find out what she's been doing and *then* let her die."

****

Rhonda heaved air into her labored lungs and nodded. She was lightheaded and nauseous and just wanted to flop. "Y...yeah, do it." It was a relief to stumble to a nearby rock, hang her head and try to stop the world spinning. Sheer terror and adrenaline had got her that far, but she suspected neither would get her any further. She put one hand over her heart and the other over her stomach, as she tried her best to slow her breathing, and stop her heart racing. It couldn't be good for the baby.

The noise of pounding feet, splashes and shouts, made her lift her head. Mac was wading out of the shallows with Marcus, still in a package. Someone she recognized, but couldn't remember his name, met them and began to tear the tape from the packaging.

Astrid sat down beside Rhonda and put her arm around Rhonda's shoulder. "Okay? What about the bump? What happened?"

"Got out through a cupboard, and followed them." She coughed and stared at Dan as he passed an unmoving Gracie over to Darke. "I think I ought to faint. I'm up shit creek without a paddle now. I was told not to move."

Astrid chuckled. "You can try, but they'll see through it, they always do. Plead pregnancy hormones. That usually works."

"Far be it from me to organize the post mortem," Dan said. "Especially on a beach at midnight, when there are much better things to be done on a beach at that hour. But how come one of my brand new darts hit the woman in the eye? Which didn't kill her, she did drown."

That was a relief. Rhonda didn't want to be responsible for killing another human, even one as evil as Gracie seemed to be.

Evil or ill? She suspected they would never know the answer to that.

"However," Dan went on. "It must have jolted her and pained her badly enough to upset her equilibrium so she stumbled backward, broke the planks, and the rest you know. So what happened to get to this?"

Rhonda managed a shaky laugh and lifted one foot in the air. The red varnished toes glistened in the moonlight. "I wanted to do my toenails while I can still see them."

Astrid giggled. "I so remember that." Darke, who had walked up to them glared. "Sorry," Astrid added. "Go on, Rhonda. You've got the stage."

She'd be happy not to have it. "Well the brush was stuck so I was looking for something pointy to try and get it loose. I found the darts and put them in my pocket. I was on my little toe, and there was a commotion outside. I remembered what Dan said, texted him, and tried to find somewhere to hide until the cavalry arrived. Well, she got into my room, so I went into a cupboard and out the back."

Dan, Darke and Astrid nodded. "The bathroom one?" Darke asked

"The very same."

"Then, love?" Dan prompted as he lifted her into his arms and sat down on another nearby rock with her cradled on his lap.

"Then I waited in the hall cupboard, hell I must like cupboards, 'til she went by. Marcus was unconscious and looked awful. How is he though?" Had they hidden the worst case scenario from her?

"He'll live, Darke said. "Battered and bruised with a few cracked ribs, but he'll live. Gracie?"

Rhonda nodded. "Gracie Elaine Frobisher."

"Gracie won't. So who is she?"

"The sister of Marcus's late wife, Lizbeth. I saw her drag Marcus onto that stuff, wrap him up and haul him down the stairs and outside. How did none of you see her?"

Darke sighed. "We did but had no idea it was Ver...your brother or who she was. Everyone on our side was accounted for. Then Mac relayed your text, said where he and Dan were and we got to the far side just in time to hear the confession. Which makes a lot of sense about all of this."

"So is it all over?" Astrid asked. "Or do you still need to find out who is really behind everything?"

Darke shrugged. "The dispatchers have disbanded. We'll never know."

Epilogue

Just over a year later
Trossachs, Scotland

"Do you know what day it is?" Rhonda asked as she sat, naked, on a cushion at the feet of Dan, her Sir and Master. "Apart from Lucie's almost two months birthday, and six months since we discovered Marcus is fine and accepted it was no one's fault, except Gracie's that Lizzie died." It had, she knew, been a painful time for her brother, but at last he seemed settled and accepted how awful things could, and did, happen to innocent people.

"Time my subbie got 'our daughter is almost two months old birthday spanking'? The one she deserves for not doing as she was told a year ago?"

"Ohh, that one?" Rhonda grinned. Their play had by necessity been softer, more gentle, and nowhere near as intense as either of them preferred. However, she'd been given the all clear to resume, as the doctor, a fellow kinkster, had said with a grin, their type of normal marital activities a few days earlier. Darke and Astrid had volunteered their holiday cottage and Astrid had happily offered to look after Lucie for the night. Neither Rhonda nor Dan thought they would cope separated from their daughter for longer than that.

"I think my Sir is right. Although I still consider it was the right thing to do, I accept I didn't do as I was told... So... I'm yours, Sir."

"Really, love?"

"Really, Sir."

"Bells, whistles, balls and chains, collared, sub, and wed mine?"

Rhonda's mouth went dry. "Ah, all of it?"

"All or nothing."

"Well I'm not sure about the whistle bit, and ball gags are a big fat red but the rest sounds good to me."

Dan laughed. "I was speaking metaphorically, but now you've explained that so delightfully, over my lap, pet. I owe you a spanking."

"Yes, Sir." She hadn't moved so fast for months.

Rhonda scrambled up and draped herself over Dan's lap. His denim clad thighs rubbed her soft skin and she wriggled a bit to increase the friction.

"Enough, or I won't spank. I'll bring you to the edge and leave you dangling there."

She stopped instantly. Dan laughed. "Works every time, pet." She scowled, happy he couldn't see her expression. He was perfectly capable of winding her up just to get a rise out of her, and they both knew it. Sometimes it would be worth it, but not now. She needed her spanking. It had been far too long since she'd achieved her happy place like that. Hot, sharp and arousing stabs of anticipation zinged from her nipples to her clit as she waited for what was to come.

Dan took her hands and placed one on each ankle, before he cuffed them, wrists to ankle.

"That is so beautiful to see, my pet. That's the chain bit. This, my dearest love, is the collar."

Something cold and thin slid around her neck. Her heart missed a beat as Dan held a mirror at the right angle so she could see the fine silver and diamond chain, which sat snug to her skin.

"Oh, Dan, Sir, it's..." she sniffed. "Perfect."

"Good." He stroked the globes of her ass one by one and she held her breath.

"Breathe, love. Are you ready?"

"Oh yes, oh my green as green yes."

"Then this is the spanking. Count, pet, and no coming until my cock is in you. A nice gentle thirty to start, a soft sweet fucking to follow."

The swats did start soft. And as she kept count got harder. Oh how she'd missed that sweet sting, which morphed into pain and gorgeous hot arousal. By ten she bit her lip, by twenty she panted, by thirty she began to sob with joy, and then...

Somehow Dan slid her off his lap and bent her back over the chair arm.

"As much as I want your ass, my pet, this time I'm going to sink my dick into your cunt so far you'll want it to stay there forever. But I'll fuck you long and hard and then, you can fly." Dan thrust into her ready pussy.

Rhonda was so, so hot, so wet, so ready for him. How the hell would she hold back her climax? "I've got to come, Sir, it's been so long, I need to fly with you." Okay it was only around nine weeks but that was a lifetime. "Please..."

"Fly, pet." Dan put one hand between them and pinched her clit as at the same time, he bent his head and bit her nipple.

It was all she needed.

With a scream loud enough to wake the neighbors—if there had been any—Rhonda tipped over the edge, vaguely aware Dan followed her.

She had no idea how long it was when she discovered she was wrapped in a blanket, and Dan held out a bottle of water and a square of chocolate. "Eat, drink."

"And be merry?" she asked as she did as he bade her.

"Hopefully. You remember I said collared and wed?"

Rhonda touched her collar. "This is all I need, Sir. I'm yours." The sense of belonging it gave her was all she ever wanted. She was his. His and Lucie's.

"Now that's a pity. Because I've got the go-ahead from Marcus to do the bended knee bit and ask you to be my wife." Dan grinned as she gaped at him. "Catching flies, love. Sadly though, the bended knee doesn't work with a subbie on it."

Rhonda twisted her head to make sure he could see how happy she was. "Ah I'll take the knee as read, then. I like it here." And her fiery ass was comfortable. "So I'll say, yes please my Sir. Let's make it complete with a ring or two."

"You me and Lucie. Has a nice sound to it. We'll spread the news." Dan grinned at her. "Tomorrow. For now, I do believe there's a rosy red ass begging to be filled. I have just the cock to fill it."

"Oh, yes, Sir."

The End

KERA FAIRE

BONUS BOOK

DEDICATION

To Nicole Plummer. I hope your book namesake is as lovely as you are, and I've done your name justice. Thanks for all your support.

KERA FAIRE

THE CONTRACT

Romance on the Go ™

Raven McAllan

Copyright © 2015

Chapter One

"Plum."

"Go away, I'm not listening." Nikki Plummer, often called Plum and she hated it, finished emptying her head-high cupboard and slammed the door—hard. Her boss moved back in a hurry to avoid her toes, knees, designer shoes, and anything else in the vicinity being pinched between the door and the jamb. Her numerous bracelets jangled as she did so, and seemed to add their displeasure to the wearer's.

"Plum, don't be silly, it was a mistake."

There it was again. Did the stupid woman have no sense whatsoever? Plum was for signing her work, nothing else. Sheesh, she'd told everyone often enough, and most people accepted it.

Not this one.

The noise of a stiletto tapping impatiently on the parquet flooring only firmed Nikki's mind up. Her boss could go to hell. The hard way. On her Manolos.

"No." *No to whatever you want. It's over.*

"You're overreacting, like I said it's all a silly mistake." There was a definite note of panic in the voice now. "Plum, stop it and listen to me."

Yeah, yours you bitch.

"No one called Plum around here." Nikki checked her desk drawer. She removed three pens, a diary, and her hot as Hades red lipstick and threw them in her kitchen sink-sized bag. Satisfied there was nothing more lurking in a corner, she grabbed her sprint from the underground—fondly known as The Clockwork Orange—ballet flats and stood up. *Anything else?* Not that she wanted or needed anyway. The rest of the stuff came with the job and could stay with it.

The feeling, the glorious feeling of liberation kicked in. Nikki zipped her bag and put on her jacket.

"Nikki, for god's sake stop this nonsense." The voice rose to a screech just one notch short of shattering glass. The panic in it was evident. "Stop being a drama queen and vying for notice." The other five or six people in the office gave up their pretense of not earwigging and listened openly.

Nikki winced at the shrill tone. "No one could ever even think of vying for attention, Geraldine, in here," she said calmly, knowing her even note and lack of concern would infuriate the other woman. "Yours or anyone else's. You command the field in that respect, even down to your own attention, weird though it sounds. Luckily I neither want nor need it. Not now. You fired me, I'm out of here."

Geraldine Butters stared at her. "I was joking."

At the back of the room someone coughed, 'bullshit'.

"You should know I didn't mean what I said. It was said in jest." Now the voice was full of panic. "Take off your jacket, put down your bag and get on with that project. I need it by the end of the month. Only you can do it."

Now we're getting to the crux of the matter. The project, whatever it is and your lack of ability. Well tough. Too bad, that's one joke that misfired on you then.

"Don't care, too late, goodbye."

"You little bitch, you'll pay for this. I gave you a job, I sorted your mess…"

That was the last straw. Nikki picked up the waste paper basket, full of sweet wrappers, old take away coffee cups as well as torn bits of paper, old train tickets, and all the detritus of a busy office and upended it over Geraldine's head.

"You can clear up this one as well then." Nikki dropped her office pass onto the desk, spun on her three-inch heels—thank goodness she could now throw them in the bin—and made her way toward the lift.

Behind her someone started to clap. She resisted the urge to high-five or curtsey. One of them needed some dignity.

"You won't get a reference," Geraldine shouted after her. "I'll see you never get a job in the business again."

"Won't need to." Nikki pressed the lift button to go down and turned to her now ex-boss. "I'm off to get me a life."

****

Six months later

Nikki grinned as she got out of the minibus, fondly nicknamed a reggae-reggae taxi by her best friend Rhonda, and waved her thanks as with a toot it sped off, Bob Marley sounding loudly from the open windows. The visit from Rhonda had been great, and they'd spent two weeks reverting to twentysomethings, sunbathing, swimming and drinking mojitos. Now she'd waved Rhonda off at the airport, and was ready to work once more.

Work in Barbados didn't have the same connotations as it did in Glasgow. For one thing her commute was ten yards by foot not ten miles by bus and tube. And she did it in sunshine and/or warm rain, not cold air and sleet. Yes, she knew that was an exaggeration, and on one of the rare, hot, sunny days you got in Scotland you wouldn't want to be anywhere else, but those days were few and far between. Here, she didn't worry if she got caught in a shower. You dried off before you got far.

Nikki crossed the road, waved her thanks at the courteous drivers who had stopped to let her pass without her fearing for life and limb, and made her way to the house she'd bought.

In reality, Geraldine had done her a favor when she threw her hissy fit, over a lack of crisps for heaven's sake, and merely brought forward Nikki's departure by a few weeks. At the time, Nikki had been biding her time, until she was certain her house was sold, her new one safely purchased and her furniture ready for storage before handing in her notice.

The sweet scent of flowers along one rampant hedgerow surrounded her as she gave a mental vote of thanks to her parents for insisting she bought a house as soon as she left uni and got a job. The gamble had paid off handsomely, and the money she'd made was enough to leave Scotland, remove to Barbados, buy her present home, and live without worry until her new business took off. Which within months, it had.

With no ghastly Geraldine around to hound her, and no suddenly thrust upon her deadlines and impossible remits, she had been able to do everything in a seemly manner and not a rush. The day she flown to Barbados once more, been handed her keys, along with a bottle of wine and a bunch of flowers to welcome her home, Nikki felt ten years had dropped off her.

Life was good.

The walk from the mini bus to her house was only a few minutes, and Nikki enjoyed the amble past the other homes, and ignored the dogs who insisted on barking as they dashed up and down the boundary fences. You'd think it would be too hot to bother. She waved to anyone around, answered a few shouted 'how are you'? and dodged the potholes in the road. Road was maybe a misnomer. The lane was generally only used by residents, and not high on the list of priorities of the roads agency. It was probably better that way and gave them peace and quiet and no bother from tourists.

"Hey girl you had a visitor." Kenna, her next door but one neighbor leaned out of a window, and winked. "He's gone but said if I saw you to say he'll be back later. If you don't want him send him my way will you? Hawt." She rolled her eyes. "You been holding out on us? Hot hunk like that hidden in your closet?" Kenna roared with laughter. "Fill me in, girlfriend, who is he?"

Hot hunk? I don't know any hot hunks, do I? No way could she count any book boyfriends.

"No idea, but if you see him around and I don't appear for a day or so it's either hot sex going on, or I'm dead. I like daisies, and you can sing 'All Things Bright and Beautiful' over my coffin."

"The little death maybe?" Kenna guffawed. She had the dirtiest laugh Nikki had ever heard.

"I should be so lucky. Ah well, I guess I can dream." Nikki sketched a wave and walked the last few yards to her gate and punched in the security code to allow her access. With hindsight, she wished she'd asked Kenna to describe the guy. Ah well he'd either come back or he wouldn't. Nevertheless, a hot guy looking for her?

That'd be right.

Maybe he wanted to avail himself of her talents? The stupid phraseology made her giggle as she unlocked her door and let herself into the cool kitchen. And maybe not. But there was no use speculating. Mr. Whoeverhewas probably had the wrong house, wanted Chestnut Avenue B instead of A. The street names were confusing. Or was looking for Marlena and Chester who used to own the property.

Instead of thinking about it, Nikki changed into a bikini, and dived into the pool, mindful that if he did come back it would be easier to answer the intercom and if necessary let him in, if she wasn't skinny-dipping. Of course she knew it would be easier still if she stayed fully clothed just in case, but blow that. It was hot, she was sticky, and she'd been looking forward to her swim for the past five hours.

The water was like a cool caress after the heat of the afternoon sun. Nikki kicked off the bottom, surfaced and did a leisurely, classy crawl from one end of the pool to the other. A decent sized pool had been one of her priorities when she went house hunting here, along with aircon, and a spare room to work in. Acorn Villa, this traditional one story house, fit every specification and more. She loved it.

Nikki jumped as high as she could and sank under the water again. Life was brilliant. Crappy bosses and commuting were a not-so-fond memory. For the sheer hell of it, Nikki laughed as she surfaced, shook her long brunette hair—now with sun-kissed streaks in it—out of her eyes...

And screamed.

The sun had gone, the air felt cooler.

The guy who stood towering over her at the edge of the pool with his shadow long enough to shade the area, exuded menace.

Hot, sex on legs, menace.

Nikki dived under the water and struck out for the other end of the pool, even though one corner of her mind said it was a futile exercise. He could pace her along the side of the pool without getting his toes wet.

How the hell had whoever it was circumvented the security system?

Who was he?

What did he want?

Damn I should have said to Kenna to come around if she saw hair or hide of him. How galling to be murdered in the pool. It'll take forever for someone to clean it out.

Chapter Two

Well that went fine and dandy—not. Ruari watched the woman, he assumed it was this Nikki Plummer he was looking for, swim effortlessly down the pool. He let her get halfway and then walked calmly toward where he assumed she'd either get out, or…or what, he had no idea.

It had seemed such a good plan when he'd thought of it. Find the bloody woman and ask her: what the hell she was playing at?

 Then demand she did what was needed.

Now he wasn't so sure. Climbing the fence had been child's play—she really needed to sort that out—but what was the Bajan punishment for breaking and entering?

His quarry surfaced a few inches from his loafer-clad feet, trod water and looked up at him.

"Who are you, what are you doing here, how did you get in?" The questions tumbled over each other. "Talk fast. My neighbor will have clocked you, and be ready to set the bloodhounds otherwise known as Henry and Arthur, both six foot plus muscle men, onto you if needed."

That he didn't doubt.

"Ruari Cameron. You owe me. I've come to collect."

"Eh?" Nikki, he was sure it was she, even if he'd only seen a photo where she was one face in a crowd, sounded totally perplexed.

"Rubbish, I do not owe anyone anything. I don't even know who you are. Now butt out and get off my property before Henry, Arthur and the local police turn up." She swam in a circle. "I'll count to ten. One…"

"Look," Ruari spoke rapidly conscious that time *was* passing and his powers of persuasion seemed to have been lost along with his suitcase somewhere between Scotland and Barbados. "Geraldine Butters sent me."

"That's a load of crap, she has no idea where I am. Plus her name is enough to ensure I'd tell you to go to hell."

"Shit, please listen, it's bloody important." He hated the neediness in his voice, but it was important she listened. "I went to get something you were supposed to have done for me, and she stalled me for weeks. Then she showed me rubbish even a six year old would baulk at. I got a bit shirty, demanded to know what game you were playing, was told you'd walked out, without finishing my commission. Just buggered off she said. No explanations. Now stupid as it may seem to you, I signed that contract with you, and expect you to fulfill it. You, Nikki Plummer aka Plum. I want a Plum job like I was promised. Not someone else, and certainly not someone with the ability of a kid who isn't interested in what she's producing. I got your address from the redhead in reception, who said no one knew what had really happened, but she bet you were blameless. Apart from the waste paper basket episode. Then she laughed so hard she got tears in her eyes, muttered something about lady pads, and dashed toward the loo. What are they, by the way? The waste paper basket and the lady pads?"

He held his hands up as she said softly "five...six..."

"Okay, okay. So I went to your house to be told you'd moved. And a very nice old lady told me where. So here I am. Begging if I have to. Without my luggage which let's face it could be anywhere by now."

"Hold on." Nikki swam to the side and gripped the edge. "I've turned the countdown off for a sec. Trust

Stephanie. The girl on reception, she's got as much nous as a pencil. Lady pads are… oh shoot, you know what they are."

He couldn't help it: he laughed at the way red color flushed her face, and she rolled her eyes. "I get the picture."

"Good, so as for luggage, it'll turn up or not. But we do have shops. Plus the urge to part tourists from their money, so that's sorted. Now, tell me, do you believe ghastly Gerry?"

"On a scale of one to ten?"

She nodded.

He shrugged. "Minus fifty I'd say, but I do need the stuff I commissioned."

She looked surprised. "Right." She heaved herself up on her hands and swung round to sit on the side of the pool. "Picture. Hmm. Weird." Water streamed off her and all over his shoes. Mindful that without his luggage all else he had to his name was a pair of flip-flops, a pair of swimming shorts, spare boxers and a clean t-shirt in his carry on luggage, all back at the hotel, Ruari took a hasty step backward.

"Sorry." The lack of sincerity was apparent.

"Accepted." He used the same tone of voice.

Nikki flushed. "So, Ruari Cameron. Who are you? What's your address and what the hell was I supposed to do for you anyway? I never signed any contract with anyone. Everything I ever did, was contracted as the firm's obligation, not a person's."

It was his turn to look surprised.

"Are you sure?" Well of course she was. "Sorry, but you've thrown me. Eight hours in a tin can with two screaming kids in the vicinity, no gluten free meal, and lost luggage does scramble your brains, I find. Someone is telling porkies. I'm rather certain it's not you, and it sure as hell isn't me. Shall we join forces and try to find out who and why?"

She bent her head back to look up at him, considering.

"I think we better. Move back if you don't want to be soaked." With one lithe movement that he admired, she stood up and grabbed a striped towel from the back of a nearby sun lounger. His brief glance of what to him seemed a perfect body, made him ache to see more.

"Right, hold on." His hostess was brisk and to the point. "Do you have your passport handy?"

"In my hotel safe."

"Which hotel?"

Ruari noticed the way she held herself. Watchful, ready and he bet, able to gouge his eyes out, or inflict a serious injury to his manhood, if she felt it necessary.

He held his hands out, palms uppermost, and named his hotel.

"Nice. Who's the manager?"

Ruari blinked. "How the hell do I know? I signed in, dropped my carry on bag, had the swiftest shower on record to try and wake up, changed out of jeans into chinos, and hot footed here."

To his surprise she smiled, and relaxed. "Okay. Well, sit in one of the chairs and give me a few minutes. I'd suggest not in the sun unless you have factor thirty handy. And get ready to tell me how you got in here."

He grinned as he chose a chair in the shade and did as she bade him. "Climbed the wall. Easy. You need a spiked top."

"I'll be onto it tomorrow," she said grimly. "Now excuse me for a sec."

"Don't get dressed on my behalf."

'I won't. I never do things unless they suit me."

That told him. Ruari chuckled, sat back into the

lounger and closed his eyes. Somewhere a bird chirruped and in the distance he could hear a green monkey calling its annoyance to someone or something. He'd forgotten how much he loved the Caribbean and Barbados in particular.

He woke up to the smell of hot strong coffee. Ruari blinked and stared at the woman who sat calmly opposite him in the dusk of a warm Caribbean evening, sipping coffee and studying him closely.

"Lord, did I fall asleep, sorry. Blame the weather at home, my lack of sleep, screaming kids, ineffective parents, and your ex-boss. In any order you want."

"Oh let's put ghastly Gerry first. The woman is a bully. Amongst other things. Here." She passed over another cup of steaming, aromatic, liquid. "I thought the smell might revive you."

"The taste will do it even better, thank you." Ruari grasped the mug and sipped the contents appreciatively. "I needed this."

Nikki regarded him over the rim of her cup. She'd tied her hair back in a careless knot, and wore a bright red sundress with tiny pearl buttons all the way down to the hem, which just skimmed her knees. Dangly pearl earrings swung from her ears, and her nails were covered in a pearly polish. Combined with her delicately tanned skin it was an arousing combination. Ruari couldn't stop his body reacting favorably, and hoped she didn't notice.

His tummy rumbled and he shook his head. "Sorry, no gluten free food on the plane. They'd," he mimed quote marks, "not received my request. And yeah pigs fly. I had an apple, three mini chocolate bars, and three slices of bacon. They offered me a pack of jam with it. I declined. I'm starving."

It was a false hope she hadn't seen the way he'd shifted in his chair. Or the way his body had altered the shape of his chinos.

"Down boy. I'm not on the menu."

Ruari swore his cheeks were the color of her dress. "Sorry, but I'm too tired to control my reactions. Luckily also too tired to act on them."

She giggled. "Don't think you might wake them up. I've trained in self defense. Oh and contacted Mike at the hotel to get verification you're who you say you are. You pass the Mike-test. By the sound of it your passport photo makes you look like a cross between a young Pierce Brosnan, Daniel Craig, and someone called Smolley. That's according to Shanaia, who checked you in." She winked. "I reckon that is not a good mix, but each to their own."

Ruari spluttered and almost choked on a mouthful of coffee. "Good grief I hope not, I'd no doubt get all their bad bits."

"Do they have any?" Nikki sniggered. "I mean Pierce and Daniel as Mr. Bond? They could play their cards right and have me."

"Smolley?"

She shook her head. "Your guess is as good as mine there. No idea who he is but evidently, according to Shanaia, he's the best thing since sliced bread and what he can't do with his hands isn't worth mentioning. I told her not to mention what he *could* do with them either and she said I needed to open my mind and live. A scary thought if a guy named Smolley and his hands are involved." Nikki rolled her eyes and grinned.

It was too much. Ruari laughed out loud, spilled his coffee all over his cream chinos and choked.

Chapter Three

Hell's bells, I hope he's not going to choke to death. Nikki stood up and thumped Ruari on the back until his choking slowed and stopped. His eyes were streaming, his chinos covered with best Jamaican brew, and he looked a mess. Her heart missed a beat and then raced. A gorgeous mess.

Oh glory, no. I do not want a complication like him in my life. No, no and NO. Damned if her heart ignored her and red hot, 'oh my I wonder what if', heat filled her. She ignored it as best she could. After all, hadn't he come to demand something of her and she had no idea what?

By the time Ruari's chest—a rather magnificent chest she judged even though it was covered in blue striped linen—stopped heaving, Nikki had her libido almost under control. *Almost.* She still had to admit he was a sight for sore eyes. And for an underused...she broke that train of thought off abruptly. She was not going to think of her lack of a sex life.

"I think maybe I'd best feed you. Food for the tummy not the soul." Nikki went into the kitchen, dampened a clean tea-towel and took it out to Ruari. "I'd say take them off and I'll shove them in a washer, but you'll need to wear a sheet or a towel if I do. I don't have any men's togs around."

"A sheet will do, I'm burning my bits off here." He dribbled the cool water from the tea-towel over his groin and sighed. "Better, much better."

She hadn't thought of that. "Then the bathroom is the third on the left. There's plenty of towels and I'll find a sheet."

Ruari disappeared at a fast waddle. His uneven

gait, she suspected, had something to do with his desire to keep hot coffee away from tender skin. Nikki followed more slowly. She wasn't sure if her reawakened sex drive could cope with Ruari in a sheet.

As she rummaged through the airing cupboard something caught her eyes. Navy...shorts... She remembered with a heartfelt sigh, just what the cotton garment was.

Shorts. Men's shorts that Rhonda used to sleep in, and had washed a few days earlier. Obviously they'd got mixed up with the sheets and pillowcases and been forgotten. But would they be big enough? She held them up, doubtfully. Ah well at least he had a choice. She took out a single sheet that she'd held on to, just in case she needed to make the sofa up for someone to sleep on, and tapped on the bathroom door.

"Yeah?" The door opened a crack and Ruari peered around it. All she could see was his head and one tanned shoulder.

Dammit a few more inches of flesh wouldn't go amiss.

"A sheet, a pair of shorts that may or may not fit, and pass me your chinos. Is your shirt okay?"

Ruari took the sheet and shorts from her and passed the trousers through the gap. "I missed my shirt. Are you sure you don't mind? I could go back to the hotel."

"Like you've been in a coffee wrestling fight and lost? After I rang Mike to vouch for you? Maybe not a good idea. There'll be enough speculation as it is, and I'd prefer not to give them fuel for any more. It'll take no time and meanwhile I'll make us something to eat."

"I'm coeliac. That means..."

"Allergic to gluten," Nikki finished for him. "Yes, I know, so am I." She bit back her grin at the astonishment on his face. "So, no cross contamination here."

She plucked his trousers out of his hands and made her way to the laundry room. Within five minutes she was in the kitchen and looking at the contents of her fridge.

Fish. It had to be. After waving Rhonda goodbye at the airport, she'd detoured to Oistins and the fish market and picked up some locally caught fish. If she cooked it with some prawns and scallops there would be more than enough for two. As long as he liked seafood. Grief, life was fraught with difficulties.

Before she second guessed herself and decided he was probably vegan or a fruitarian the man in question reappeared.

Hot damn. He'd fitted into the shorts, but they didn't leave a lot to the imagination. Or, Nikki decided, much room to breathe. Thank goodness he'd left his shirt loose, and the hem of it covered most of his groin.

He grinned self-consciously, as Nikki dragged her eyes upward, away from what she now decided was the danger zone.

"Yeah well, I decided I'd rather cut my…" he paused and winked, "circulation off than fall flat on my face and do untold damage to whichever bits of me met the floor first." He looked at the fish she held in her hands and groaned appreciatively.

"Mahi-Mahi?"

Nikki nodded. "Do you like it? I thought with prawns and scallops."

Ruari sighed theatrically, and put his hand over his heart. "Be still my throbbing heart. Mahi-mahi, and seafood. Oh god, I'm in heaven. Will you marry me?"

Nikki ignored the way her tummy got butterflies, the rest of her insides quivered, and her mushy brain went *yes please*. The guy still thought she'd diddled him somehow. "Not just so I can have your gratitude because I cook you fish for the rest of your life, no." She seasoned the food, added wine and butter, wrapped it in tinfoil and placed it in the heated oven.

"Oh there would be more benefits than my thanks for your cooking," Ruari drawled.

Where was cool air when you needed it? If it hadn't looked so obvious, Nikki would have fanned herself with a tea-towel. Instead she opened the fridge and stuck her head inside its chilled interior. Did he know what those words did to her? A swift glance around the fridge door at his face told her that of course he did.

How on earth can you react so intensely to someone you've only just met?

"I feel it as well, you know. Scary, isn't it?"

"Wine?" Nikki asked and hoped the wobble in her voice was too slight to be obvious. "I have a New Zealand sauvignon."

"Why not, thank you. It won't take too long to stagger back to the hotel."

So he's not going to try and get me to let him stay, then?

The swift sharp stab of disappointment that ran through her like a fast flowing river surprised her as much as it amazed her. She'd never been one for instant attraction and snap decisions but if he gave even half an inkling he wanted her she'd be on her knees and begging.

The pictures that scenario conjured up did nothing to help cool her skin, just the opposite. Nikki counted to ten, and backed out of the fridge holding the bottle she needed.

"Can you take this outside please? Cooler and glasses in the cupboard by the door." She thrust the bottle at Ruari, who thankfully took it.

"Sure, anything else."

"Er no thanks, not at the moment."

Just go. Check out the humming birds, rearrange the glider cushions. Cut the grass with scissors. Anything, just get out of my sight for a few minutes.

Anything to give her a bit of breathing space.

He nodded and she swore he said, "or else I'll jump you," but surely she was mistaken? Nikki had never thought of herself as jumpable. Approachable, fun, and not too shabby in bed, but not jumpable.

Maybe she'd been wrong all these years.

And maybe pigs *could* fly. With a silent snigger at the way her thoughts flitted about, Nikki got out the makings of a salad.

"I think we need to get this over and done with you know." The knife was taken from her hands and put on the work surface and Ruari spun her around to face him.

"We're both circling around it. This attraction." He elaborated on his statement, as she was sure she stared at him as if he had two heads. "So I reckon if we do this now..." Ruari held onto her shoulders and pulled her toward him until their bodies touched. "Yes?" One eyebrow was raised in query.

She swallowed heavily. How to reply without sounding like a needy Nora?

"Why not." There, did that have the correct depth of interest? Surely it was better than punching the air and shouting 'hell yes, hurry up' at the top of her voice?

He gave a deep sexy laugh that made her toes curl and her insides go to mush. "Why not indeed." His lips touched hers and Nikki lost all coherent thought.

She had no idea how long it was before the earth

stopped spinning, and Ruari drew back and swiped his finger gently over her swollen lips. "I knew it would be good," he said and cleared his throat. "But, bloody hell, that was more than good. I'm hooked."

Okay, now she'd believe it when Rhonda told her that every time George kissed her, the earth moved. Or when Kenna said one look from Henry and she was putty.

Nikki blinked. "Um…" Gah, now *she* sounded like a six year old. "Hooked?"

"Caught, hook, line and sinker. Want to try again and see if you feel the same way?"

Was the man mad? Didn't her lack of coherence ´ tell him anything? Mind you…

"Well, why n… oh shoot, the fish." A pungent odor hit her nostrils and she whirled away to open the oven door. Smoke billowed out and she swore. "Damn it… no hold on, pass me the oven gloves please." She held her hand out and Ruari gave her the thick padded cloth. Nikki bit her lip and then giggled. "Remind me never to be distracted when I cook, and to always check the oven before I turn it to high." She withdrew a charred and smoking dish, its contents impossible to decipher and wrinkled her nose. "*Voila*, the culprit."

Ruari wafted the smoke away and peered in the direction of what she held. Nikki noticed he didn't get too close. Sensible man.

"Er what is, or should I say what was it? It doesn't look much like fish to me."

"Was. It was the remains of a shepherd's pie. It is now, I suspect, of no use to anyone let alone shepherds."

Ruari glanced at it once more and shook his head slowly.

"RIP shepherd's pie. And the dish?"

"And the dish. The dish is no more. Bin, here we

come."

"Lead the way." He stood up and made his way to the door, as Nikki shut the oven and began to follow him.

"Left out of the door, next to the garage."

"Hey." Ruari turned around to face her, and kissed her cheek. "Isn't it lucky I took the wine outside? I've never liked oaked and smoky Chardonnay. I reckon smoky Sav Blanc would be even worse."

Chapter Four

Nikki's giggle was infectious. Ruari bit back his own chuckle and opened the metal dustbin for her to deposit the late lamented pie and dish in it. He had a thought. "Maybe dunk it in water first? So it doesn't set fire to your bin and contents?"

"Sheesh, you have befuddled me. How on earth did I forget that?" Nikki dropped the dish on the ground and used a watering can to cover it with liquid. The dish hissed and sizzled for several minutes before she prodded it with the rose of the can.

"I reckon that will do." However, Ruari was pleased to note, she still used the oven gloves to lift it up and deposit it in the metal receptacle.

"Right." Nikki put the oven gloves over her shoulder. Her eyes twinkled with mischief. "Where were we?"

"About to save the fish and then you were going to let me kiss you senseless."

"I was?"

Ruari nodded. "You were."

"Hmm. I thought you'd done the kissing senseless thing already?"

He nodded. "And I want to do it again. And again." His tummy rumbled, and to his amusement, hers copied his. "But maybe after we've eaten. Although not of course on a full stomach."

"Can't win," Nikki rolled her eyes dramatically. "Okay a light dinner, another senseless kissing, and a chat."

He pinched her bum and she squealed. "Sorry, couldn't resist it." he said. "You have what my sister calls a choochy bum."

"Fat?"

"No the sort of butt you want to stroke. And pinch when you diss my kisses. Let me tell you, my kisses are never senseless, woman. The very thought."

She rolled her eyes. *God she's good at that.* The emotions that one gesture could convey were legion. Ruari was enjoying himself. All he could hope was when he fessed up she'd still treat him the same.

"They might render you senseless, in fact I hope they do, but they are *not* senseless. Note the difference." He pulled her closer and pressed his mouth firmly over hers, teasing her lips with his tongue until they softened enough to let him slip it between them and into her mouth.

She put her arms around his waist and moaned into him. The sensuous sound resonated through him, and his body once more responded to a siren call and hardened to the point of pain. He had to hope the hotel had a never ending supply of cold water for a shower. Somehow, Ruari thought he might need it, just so he didn't give in to the urge to take her there and then.

She's mine. The thought shook him. They hardly knew each other, but somehow, those words rang true.

He gentled the embrace, ended the kiss with more reluctance than he'd thought imaginable, and dropped his forehead onto the top of her head. "Senseless?" he asked in a teasing tone.

"Sense losing. In the nicest possible way. Oh shoot, the bloody fish." Nikki whirled away and ran inside. "You pour the wine." She was back outside even before he'd filled both glasses. "Saved. We have around ten minutes, before it's cold fish. Mind you I still have to make a salad. I sort of got distracted." She took the glass he offered her and clinked it to his. "Cheers. Oh and another thought. Mozzy repellant. Do you want some?"

Her mind flitted about fast enough to make a man without sisters giddy. Luckily, Ruari thought, he had three and was well versed in the way a woman's mind worked. "No need for salad. Let's just chop a tomato up and bung it on the side of the plate. Live dangerously without our five a day. I never get bitten, much to my sisters' disgust. I have three," he added before she could ask. "Ella, Tara and Susan. I'm the youngest. I'm sure Dad breathed a sigh of relief when I turned out to be a boy. He always said lassies are so thrawn you never know what's coming next. Don't ask me to explain I never did really understand what he meant."

"Perverse."

Ruari laughed. "And more. Those three could make even the most logical thing seem illogical. However I love them all. And their husbands and my, at the last count, ten, almost eleven, nieces and nephews."

"Eleven? Gracious."

"Ella has twin boys and a girl, Tara three girls and Susan two of each, and one about due now. Sex unspecified. Us males are rooting for a boy to even the numbers up a bit."

"You do know it's the male who determines the sex of a child, don't you?'

Ruari spluttered into his wine. She had a way of saying the most outrageous things so deadpan it hit you with the force of a frying pan in the gut. *And that is a stupid comparison. She's fried your brains as well as the fish.* Okay, she hadn't actually fried the fish, but he knew what she meant.

"Yes, even I did basic biology."

"*Even* you?"

Trust her to pick up on that.

"I was more of an arts student." Ruari hoped that was suitably detailed enough for her. He really wasn't ready to spill the beans just yet.

"Really, what sort?"

"A good one. Right let's get this fish out eh?"
Plus change the subject.

"Damn yes, see you're at it again. Addling me."

He hoped so. "I'll chop the tomato."

"You set the table. The stuff is in the drawer next to the outside kitchen sink. Food in three."

It was less than that. Ruari had hardly sorted out the cutlery before Nikki appeared with two plates, and explained she'd just halved the food and was that all right. She'd also managed a neat salad on each plate as well.

"Very all right."

"In fact," he said ten minutes later, "more than very all right. Spot on in fact."

Nikki smiled. "Good." She yawned and put her hand over her mouth. "Sorry. My best mate just left today and after two weeks of late nights and early mornings. I'm shattered."

He took the hint.

"Then let me wash up and I'll leave you to go to bed." He didn't ask if she wanted company, brushed off her halfhearted protests that she could clear up after he'd gone, and made short shrift of scouring the pots and pans. Half an hour later he found himself outside the gate, with a promise from Nikki that she'd sort the fence, check her doors were locked, and pick him up from outside his hotel at five the following morning to take him to a favorite vantage point and see the sunrise. As he'd slept through the sunset, and it was in his mind already almost dawn, he made a mental note to ask for a wake up call and set his phone alarm.

Satisfied that he'd met, and spent time with Nikki, and she really still had no idea why he was there, Ruari made his way back to his beachfront hotel and then to bed.

Five o'clock came much too soon and the receptionist who gave him his wake up call was way too cheery for the time of night. Or was it morning? Whichever, she had an upbeat note in her voice that he'd be hard pressed to find after midnight, let alone well into a night shift.

Ruari shoved a disc in the coffee machine and heard the welcome glug of water as it began to do its job. He showered whilst it was brewing, drank it in three gulps and nigh on scalded his tongue as he did so. Then he made his way to the lobby and out into the predawn chill.

Thank goodness for a fleece. It might be twenty odd degrees warmer than Scotland, but at silly o'clock it was still chilly enough for sleeves. Why had he teamed his cozy top with shorts and sandals? Crazy. He hoped Nikki wouldn't be long, and her car had heating as well as aircon. Ruari scanned the road in the direction he thought Nikki would come.

Nothing. Not even a stray dog.

A roar like a 747 coming into land made him look skyward. Surely it was too early for planes to land.

Apart from a few stars twinkling the sky was clear. No clouds and definitely no plane. The roar got louder, and he turned around to see a very large Harley zoom into the car park and stop in front of him.

The visor lifted. "Helmet." She handed a bright red helmet to him. "Hop on. Sorry I'm a few minutes late, I forgot the camera." The visor flipped down again and she revved the engine and stared at his legs.

"Shorts?" Nikki shrugged. "Ah well, we won't be on it too long." She revved the engine once more.

Ruari took the hint, donned the helmet and

climbed onto the bike behind her. He'd barely got settled before she put the machine into gear and moved off, way too fast in his opinion. At least it gave him a good excuse to put his hands around her waist.

"You'd be safer holding the back of the seat."

Nikki seemed to speak directly into his helmet. Ruari found his mouthpiece. "Not half as much fun though."

She snorted and increased the speed. They roared past the entrance to Graham Hall Gardens and he hoped she'd remembered the police station was around the corner.

She had. The bike slowed and kept to a decorous speed until they passed the airport several miles further on. They obviously hadn't used the main road, and with the lack of signposts and twists and turns, Ruari had no idea where they were going.

"So, are we heading to Crane?" He remembered his geography. Plus one of the few signposts he saw and was able to read indicated it was in the direction they were headed.

"No, nor Bathsheba, wait and see."

He didn't really have much option. Ruari settled back to enjoy the ride. Twenty minutes later, Nikki turned the bike onto a bumpy track, and drove slowly along it, missing the deepest of the dips and holes. She pulled up by a bush, and cut the engine.

Ruari got off and waited until she locked the bike and took off her helmet.

With a grin Nikki shook her head. "Gah, helmet hair. The worst ever. Come on, we go down here, we should be just in time. Watch these steps. They're wooden and splintered." She slung on a backpack she'd taken out of a pannier, added their helmets to the space, locked it and set off two steps at a time. Ruari hurried after her. Obviously she didn't think the warning applied to her own descent.

He arrived, breathless, on the sand at the bottom of the steps scant seconds after her.

"Woman, do you have a death wish? You took those at a reckless speed." Ruari panted as he tried to get his breath back. The last twenty or so steps were steep, broken and lethal.

She laughed. "Pot kettle and black, mate. I know them, what's your excuse?"

She had a point.

"Worry, and sheer blue funk."

"Never mind, we can go back up slower. Quick, make for that rock over there and be prepared to be gobsmacked." She pointed to a rock, which stood near the water's edge and set off across the sand at a speed Ruari decided he'd be hard pressed to achieve on tarmac let alone fine soft sand.

She thrust a bottle of water at him once he gained the top of the rock and looked out to sea. Already the sky was light enough to see the faint glimmer of the sun just below the horizon.

"Do you have a camera?"

He nodded, too out of breath to speak, and took it out of his pocket. It was only small but it did as he wanted.

"Right, enjoy then. Don't get so carried away with framing your shots you forget to look and wonder." Nikki dropped to her knees and stretched out on her stomach facing the east.

She was correct: it was something to wonder over. On this coast the gentle waves that washed the sands outside his hotel were bigger and bolder, with white crests and crashing descents. Within seconds Ruari had dropped his hand to his side and just stared. First pink and dark blue streaks appeared above the rollers, then yellow and crimson began to tinge the pale blue sky. Gradually the warmth of the sun made its presence known. At first slowly, then ever faster, like a rose unfurling or a new baby opening its eyes on the world, the golden orb presented itself in all its glory.

Ruari stared until his eyes hurt. "That," he said at last, "was magnificent. Thank you. And you were right, it was better to look and wonder than have my eye glued to the camera."

Nikki nodded. "Every time, and even though I'm used to it I never get used to it if you get my meaning? Right, breakfast. Grab this bag for me while I go get our table."

"Table?"

She was already scrambling off the rock and rummaging under the overhang they'd stepped over to gain the flat top he still stood on.

"Wait and see."

He was asked to do lot of that. With a wry grin, after all it was usually he who gave the orders, Ruari bent his legs and perched on his ass. The stone—rock was a bit of a misnomer—in all honesty, it wasn't more than a couple of feet high and three across. Big overlarge lump was perhaps a better description. However the few feet he'd gained in height had been perfect. Now he wanted to return for another dawn and take in the view from ground—or sand—level.

"Grab this." Nikki's head and arms appeared over the edge, as she handed up a thin piece of wood, around a foot across and an inch thick. "*Voila* our table. It fits over that dip." She scrambled back up to perch next to him and waited for Ruari to fix the wood as she directed, before rummaging in her backpack again.

"Right, G-f rolls, jam—cos I hate cheese—pate,

in case you hate jam, and coffee. How's that? Just to keep us going until we get to Mama D's."

"Mama D's?"

"Wait and see."

There were those words again. She really needed to up her vocabulary. However, Ruari wouldn't moan. The thought of sustenance was good one.

"I'm in your hands," he said amiably.

"You so are, and I love it." She twirled an imaginary moustache. "You will do as I sa...ay.... Well maybe. Anyway coffee?"

They sat in companionable silence and munched away, as the sun rose and the heat increased. Once they'd finished the bottle of water Nikki produced after the coffee, she stretched like a contented cat. "Ready for the next leg?"

"Hmm. Maybe. How private is this beach?"

Nikki stopped packing her bag and looked up at him curiously. "For the next hour or so, very. Why?"

"Well, I think this might be a good time to..." He took Nikki by the shoulders and pulled her to lie flat next to him. "Do this."

Chapter Five

All her breath whooshed out of her, as her back hit the rock, luckily over the blanket. Knobbly rock digging into your back wasn't conducive to anything at all.

Especially if he intended what she hoped he did. "Um what?" *Duh, eloquence thy name is not Nikki.*

He grinned, and leaned over her. "Maybe this?"

Once more Nikki lost her breath as Ruari's lips met hers. Why on earth was something that in some ways was so insignificant so important? That made her shiver and shake and want more. Not jut a kiss on the lips but a kiss elsewhere?

Nikki met his tongue with hers and gladly let them mesh and tease. She tried to rear up and touch him, but he stopped her by simply putting his hand on her shoulder.

"No." Ruari broke the kiss. "Not yet. Not until you're ready."

What? "I am ready." Nikki opened her eyes and looked him in the face. The tender expression on his face made her insides go all gooey again. "Truly, I am," she protested.

"Without knowing why I'm here?"

Damn she'd forgotten that. "Okay, so tell me."

"No, not yet. I want another kiss first."

"I want more than that," Nikki said, and winced at the sulky tones she heard herself use. "Ah, knickers, sorry. Mump alert. Here." She pressed her lips to his quickly drew back and ran her fingers over his cheek. "Okay, there's your kiss. Next step."

He laughed. "Talk about determined."

She nodded. "You better believe it. Grief, I've not felt so revved up for ages, and you're determined to turn my motor off again."

Ruari, snorted. "A Harley or a Maserati?"

Nikki giggled. "Take your pick."

"My pick is you. But not until I tell you why I'm here."

"You did. I didn't do something you thought I should have done and I know I shouldn't. Now you won't do something I think you should, because you think you shouldn't."

"Clear as mud."

"Exactly. Ignore it." She did her best to look sultry, but knowing her, she probably just looked constipated. "I have. Can we not just enjoy ourselves and worry about stuff later?"

Was it really her who was saying such things? Coming on so strong it was a wonder Popeye wasn't handing over his spinach. The silence lengthened.

"Ah forget it, let's go and have breakfast. Then you can yell at me, I can slap your face, you can clear off and life can go back to normal."

And if I believe that, you can sell me a bridge.

"Not a chance. Do you mean it? That you want me without knowing why I'm here?"

"Oh yes. I mean it, your body wants it…" She looked over to where his shorts were tented. "So?"

"So, never let it be said I disappoint a lady. Lie down."

Nikki shrugged off her jacket, rolled it into a ball to use as a pillow, and complied with alacrity. If he didn't get a move on they'd be mid bonk when the local fishermen arrived.

She wriggled to get into the most comfortable position she could find. Ruari laughed softly. "You wriggle so well."

"Good, what do you do well?"

"This." He flicked open the buttons of her shirt and slid the two sides apart. Never had Nikki been so pleased she hated bras and hadn't bothered to wear one.

"And this." He bent over her, took one hard nipple into his mouth and suckled. She arched her back and silently begged for more. She had two nipples dammit and one was feeling neglected.

Ruari lifted his lips and blew on the damp nub before he turned his attention to the other one.

Dimly Nikki felt his hands at her waist and then warm air feathered over her tummy as the zip of her denims was lowered.

"Lift up." He put one hand under her bum and tugged the soft denim downward until only her thong was between her butt and the blanket.

Nikki had an awful thought. How would he get her jeans over her boots?

The answer was simple, he didn't even try. He left the material bunched around her knees, effectively holding her in one position.

"Ah now what a beautiful sight. Tell me are you sure about this?"

She nodded. "Condom in the pocket of my back pack."

He shook his head.

No?

"No? Why not?" Damn him he couldn't leave her so excited and not bring her to a climax, surely? There was not a snowball's chance in hell she was going to let him anywhere near her without one

"Condom in the back pocket of my jeans. I live in hope."

Whew. Nikki shoved her hands into the pocket

he'd mentioned, with more speed than finesse, and withdrew a foil packet.

"Bingo."

He laughed, turned over onto his back, stretched out next to her and undid the laces on his shorts. As the waistband slackened and he pushed it lower, his erection sprang free and to Nikki's overheated imagination, waved hello. Or was it 'I'm coming to get you?' Whichever, it was impressive and she gulped. Ripped open the foil before she chickened out and left them both frustrated, and looked Ruari in the eye.

"May I?"

"Yeah." He seemed to be too concentrated on his breathing to say any more.

With as much care as her fumbling fingers allowed, Nikki pushed his shorts down further, rolled the condom onto his staff and smoothed it across the hard length.

Ruari groaned. "Enough I want to come inside you, not like this." He moved in one swift movement, kicked off his shorts somehow, and positioned himself over her.

"Ready?"

Nikki nodded. Her mouth was too dry and her breath too erratic to speak. Instead she moved her hands, grasped him, guided him to the entrance of her channel and lifted her hips. If that wasn't obvious enough, then she'd give up and go fishing.

That thought made her grab his shoulders, and urge him on.

Fishing.

Fisherman.

For goodness sake do it now. She was sure she hadn't spoken out loud, so Ruari must be good at reading body language.

He surged into her, waited for a second, looked at her face tenderly, and then obviously reading her approval in her expression, he began to move.

With her legs trapped by her jeans and with Ruari over her and in her, the friction on her body was intense. Every nerve end was on edge, every little movement higher, deeper and attacked her senses more than usual.

Nikki lifted her arms, and ran her fingers around his nipples. The swirls of hair around the areolae teased her fingertips and directed her hands lower, to follow the arrow of springy curls that lead downward.

"Enough, I'm going to..." Impossible as it seemed, Nikki decided he filled her even more, felt bigger, harder, and longer as he increased his pace.

When he stretched down, put one hand between them and touched the sensitive bundle of nerves hidden by her pubic hair, Nikki lost any coherent thoughts she had and flew. Tumbled into a rainbow of colors. Lights flashed behind her eyelids and she shivered, shook and let sensations lead her ever deeper into her climax.

Dimly she heard Ruari shout his release and then slump over her, his chest heaving and his breath choppy.

The silence was almost absolute. If you discounted harsh breathing, and waves crashing on the shore. If she had the energy she could have chuckled. Talk about a chick-flick movie moment.

Instead, Nikki touched the back of Ruari's neck with slow gentle strokes, the most contented she'd ever been in her thirty-four years. Gradually, her breath regained a near normal pace and she sighed.

Ruari levered himself onto his elbows and looked down at her. "That bad? Or am I squishing you?"

"Neither, I'm contented. That was a sated, satisfied and about to go into the oh my goodness I hope it was as good for you as it was for me, mode, sigh."

"Better."

"Impossible. I get first dibs on better." Nikki, giggled and Ruari raised his eyebrows.

"You do that and you'll shake me out of you faster than I entered."

She looked over his shoulder at the outline of the cliffs, partly shadowed by the angle of the sun, glanced at the level of the waves and looked at her watch.

"Sheesh, if we don't get a move on, we'll be more than satisfied etcetera. We'll be front page news of the local rag. Judging by the tide, it's almost fishermen time. er..." She wriggled and Ruari took the hint. He lifted himself off her, out of her and rolled to her side.

"So no time to go skinny-dipping then?"

"Nope." *More's the pity.* There was nothing better than the soft silkiness of water on bare skin. "I can offer you a wet wipe though." She dug into the backpack, pulled out a packet of the moist tissues, took one for herself and handed the packet over.

By the time, she'd used the cloth to tidy herself, amazed at her boldness in front of him, Ruari had achieved the same aim and had pulled his shorts up. He smiled ruefully.

"Another time?"

"Hopefully. Right, let me wriggle back into these denims and we'll make tracks to Mama D's." Why did your jeans always seem so much tighter when you need to dress in a hurry? By the time she'd pulled them up, zipped them and re-buttoned her blouse she was sweating. Voices floated across from the direction of the steps and she breathed an exaggerated sigh of relief. "Phew, just in time. Come on."

She stood up and reached for the backpack. Ruari shook his head.

"If that's locals and you know them?" His voice

rose to question her.

"Probably."

"Then no way am I letting you carry that. They'd probably lynch me for being less than a man."

Nikki stared at him. He winked. She burst out laughing. "Well I could reassure them over that but...maybe I'll just let you carry the bag. Much less complicated."

"Yeah. Now didn't you mention food?"

They'd jumped down from the rock and were half way across the sands, hand in hand and at a much more decorous pace than they'd covered the distance earlier, when three elderly gentlemen appeared at the entrance to the track, carrying fishing rods and stools. As the two parties met, one waved his rod in the air.

"Hellooo, it's my baby Nikita. How's it going honey?" He stared at Ruari. "Who's this then?"

Nikki grinned and flung her arms around the man and gave him a hug and a kiss, which the man reciprocated with fervor.

"Papa D, it's all cool. Meet Ruari, a friend from Scotland." Ruari stuck his hand out and papa D took it.

"Honeychil', you got a man at last eh?"

Sheesh, why wouldn't the sand open up and swallow her?

Chapter Six

"Ruari Cameron, and I live in hope." Ruari took pity on Nikki and deflected Papa D's attention.

Papa D shook his head. "Baby, you aren't getting any younger. Here's this fine looking man after you and you not jumping him? Baad." He tapped Nikki's nose. "You get stuck in there while he's still after your body."

She was, Ruari realized embarrassed, but struggling not to laugh. A right mix.

"I'll think about it."

"You do that my girl, and let me cuddle your babe before I go to meet my maker." He turned his head, grinned and winked at Ruari, who couldn't help but wink back at the man's audacity.

"Now you off to mama for breakfast? She must have known you'd be around, I smelt oat and banana muffins."

"Papa D you are a bad man. I won't tell mama this time, but..." Nikki wiggled her finger. "I'll eat all the muffins instead."

"You would, but Hector, Dwayne and I? We got some in our bags. See here, Ruari man, she needs a firm hand. Maybe on her butt and all if she mouths off at you."

"Papa D. What would mama say if she heard you talk like that?" Nikki said in a voice full of mirth.

"Whip my butt, but she's not here. Now off you go, and let a man catch his tea."

As soon as the men were out of earshot, Ruari burst out laughing. "If you could have seen your face. I'm guessing you know him well?"

"Since I was born. Mama looked after me whilst my mum taught at the local school. Outed, I'm actually

Bajan. Mum reckons her ancestors were descended from pirates and dad's from the first British Governor. We lived here until I was twelve and then moved to Glasgow so Dad could lecture at the uni. I came back as soon as I knew I could support myself."

"So, do you live in your parents' house?" Ruari loved the way she was beginning to open up. Perhaps his demand wouldn't be too over the top after all.

They reached the bike once more, and prepared to set off.

"Nah, it's mine, all mine, well, with a hefty mortgage. Mum and Dad still have their house, of course. They're due to come back when Dad retires, allegedly next year. I'll believe it when I see it, mind. No, their house isn't very far from the Crane. I prefer the bustle and beach at Rockley. Okay? Are you ready to be inspected, dissected and fattened up?"

"You make me sound like a pig."

"You'll feel like one by the time you've finished eating what Mama D puts in front of you."

Thank goodness he had an elasticated waistband to his shorts.

An hour later Ruari decided never had truer words been spoken. Mama D had hugged him, quizzed him—although with a lot more finesse than her husband—and pronounced him one to keep, not one to throw back.

Ruari decided he'd never have the need to blush again.

As they left she patted his cheek. "You bring my baby back soon. And get her off that death trap she insists on riding eh?"

"I'll do my best Mama D," Ruari said as they left the tiny café.

"Don't you go siding with her." Nikki swung her

leg over the bike and switched it on. "My life, my bike."

"I accept that, but think of what we can get up to in a car if it rains."

"Depends on the car."

True enough. He put his arms around her and enjoyed the ride back to Rockley. To his surprise, Nikki turned the bike into the beach front car park, cut the engine and took off her helmet.

"Want to walk the boardwalk? Walk and talk on neutral ground?" she asked as she took his helmet from him and locked it up with hers. She fluffed up her hair and stuck the keys in her blouse pocket. "You tell me why you're here and let me see if I can make head or tail of it?"

"Why not." He waited whilst she took off her boots, locked those away as well and rolled up her jeans. "Aren't you hot in denims?"

Nikki struck a pose. "Oh sugar, Ah do hope so." Then she laughed. "Seriously, no self respecting Bajan would say jeans are too hot. You get used to it. As you do going barefoot. It freaked everyone when we moved to Scotland and the soles of my feet were like leather. I only wear shoes if I really must. Bare feet or flip flops all the way."

Ruari took off his sandals and followed her across the sand, amused as she detoured to a kiosk, disappeared inside it and emerged a minute later with a carrier bag, and wearing a sarong.

Nikki winked. "I still hate jeans when it's hot, but woe betide me admitting it to any Bajan friends. Lulu is a mate. I've blagged some water as well." She waved the carrier. "She'll hold on to my jeans for me until later." With a grin, she retraced her steps to the sand, and carried on walking over it.

It was hot but still bearable. Within a few hours it

wouldn't be possible to saunter, more like hop from foot to foot. Ruari remembered her earlier statement about footwear.

"Bare feet, even on this sand?"

"Even then. Right, best foot forward, let's strut our stuff. Of course it should be sunset or we should have pedometers and a serious expression, but me, I'll settle for slow, sensible and enjoyment every time."

"Definitely." Ruari waited until they'd left the sand and gained the boardwalk. It was busy, but not overcrowded. A favorite place for anyone of all ages, shapes, and sizes to do their own thing. There were people with dogs, pushing buggies, running, power walking and sauntering, in groups, couples and alone.

"Every combination imaginable," Ruari said as they skirted three teenagers who surely should have been in school, a tot on a trike, and an incredibly overweight man hefting what looked like a can of beans in each hand as he walked.

"I love it." Nikki led him along a tiny headland to sit on the wall at the end. Nobody was within five yards of where they sat. "Okay, let's get it over with. What do you want, and why? Apart from my body of course."

"That's a given. That I want your body. I also want your other talent."

She titled her head to one side and opened her eyes wide. "Which one? I have several. For instance I can hold a pencil between my upper lip and my nose. Write with my left foot. Ride a bike backward...ooft." Ruari put his hand over her mouth.

"I look forward to seeing them all. The one I'm talking about it's the way you turn a photo into a picture. Like the cover of my last album." He waited to see what she would say or do.

After she'd stared at him for several seconds and

not said a word he continued. "And the next one, which I contracted to Butters's because I was promised would be a Plum job. "

"You what?" She stared at him closely. "Oh my giddy blooming goodness. Shit, and I don't swear. Apricot Kisses. I was so proud of that cover. You're Ru Cameron. Damn it how did I not know?" She put her head in her hands. "Go away. I'm so bloody embarrassed."

Ruari tugged her hands away and put her onto his lap. She didn't move off, so he hoped that was a positive sign. He rubbed his chin. "No guitar in my hands or across my back? No beard? Shorter hair? You weren't expecting me?"

"All of those."

"I'm fatter, thinner, older than you remember?"

"I've never met you before. Last year, ghastly Gerry conveniently forgot to tell me about the award ceremony until I'd booked my holiday here. And reminded me that it was the firm who took the kudos and the honors, not an individual. I've never even touched the trophy."

"Bitch."

Nikki nodded. "You said it. So you were expecting me to do another one? That was why she freaked when I walked?"

"I'll bet. She'd promised me it would be another Plum job. I hit the roof when it wasn't. Luckily, the contract was signed as I'd detailed so she got short shrift. I lied when I met you."

"Why?"

Ruari kissed her nose, enchanted when she wrinkled it. "I still wasn't one hundred percent sure you hadn't just run out on the assignment. Not until I met you."

"And now?"

"And now I know that ghastly Gerry is exactly that. Ghastly. And a bloody chancer. It might please you to know, she isn't doing so well. A fair few have jumped ship."

"Ah well, karma always bites you on the bum." Nikki kissed his cheek. "What shall we do without karma?"

Ruari kissed her back, harder and longer.

"Woot, maan, get youse a room, eh?" The whistle that accompanied the words, made them draw apart and laugh.

"Sounds good to me," Ruari said. "What say you?"

"Yeah, but first. Do you still want your next cover to be a Plum job?"

Ruari stood up and she slid off his lap. "I'd love it. But even just after a day of knowing you, I want more." He tucked her arm into his and turned back toward the bike, the beach and his hotel. With a nice air conditioned room in it.

"I want my life to be a Plum job. My home, my kids, my everything. Shall we draw up a contract?"

"Well now…" For three long heartbeats Nikki was silent. His throat closed up. Had he blown it?

"I think we need to negotiate," she said huskily. "How long were you thinking this contract should last?"

"Hmm. A lifetime maybe?"

"Deal. You've got yourself a Nikki, for ever. Your very own Plum job."

The End

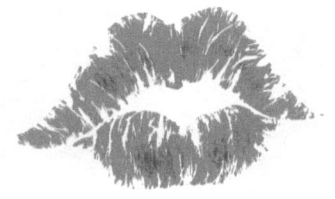

EVERNIGHT PUBLISHING ®

www.evernightpublishing.com